GROUND
ZERO

Also by Alan Gratz

ALAN GRATZ

GROUND ZERO

SCHOLASTIC INC.

ISBN 978-1-338-86515-8

12 11 10 9 8 7 6 5 4   23 24 25 26 27

Printed in the U.S.A.   40

Originally published in hardcover by Scholastic Press, February 2021

This edition first printing, September 2022

Book design by Yaffa Jaskoll

For Jennifer Hull Price

BRANDON

HOW WE SURVIVE

Brandon Chavez was in trouble.

He *should* have been in school this morning, taking his seat by the window and sharing a new skateboarding magazine with his friends. Instead, he sat next to his dad on a crowded subway train, heading from Brooklyn into Manhattan.

Brandon wasn't allowed to go to school today.

He was suspended.

SHOOM. Brandon jumped as the train burst from its underground tunnel into the full light of day for its climb to the Manhattan Bridge. It was a bright, blue, clear September morning, and he squinted from the sudden sun.

Beside him, his father folded up the newspaper he'd been reading.

"Okay, Brandon, when are we going to talk about this?"

Brandon didn't want to talk about getting suspended. He hadn't talked during dinner last night, or at breakfast this morning, or while he and his dad had waited for the subway. Now Brandon could *feel* the silence, like an invisible thing that had squeezed in between them on the seat and was pushing them apart.

His dad turned to face him. Leo Chavez wasn't a big man, but he had a stocky chest and strong arms. Brandon thought he would have made a good professional wrestler. There was a quiet power in his dad, and Brandon could feel that power directed at him now.

"I get a call at work from your school, and I'm thinking, is Brandon sick? Did he crack his head open again doing stunts on the playground?" his dad said. "But no. They're calling to tell me my son punched another kid in the nose."

"He deserved it!" Brandon said. All his anger and frustration from yesterday came flooding back as he turned to his father. "Cedric brought these Wolverine gloves to school, like from the *X-Men* movie? And Stuart Pendleton stole them and wouldn't give them back!"

"So you punched Stuart in the nose."

"He wasn't going to give them back! What was I supposed to do?"

Brandon's dad sighed. "I don't know, Brandon. *Talk* to him. Tell a teacher or something."

Talk to him? You couldn't talk to a bully like Stuart Pendleton! And telling a teacher might have gotten Cedric his gloves back, but Stuart would have just beaten Brandon up later for tattling.

"*You don't understand,*" Brandon told his dad.

"I understand enough to know that punching him wasn't the answer," his dad said. "And the principal told me that this other boy you were trying to help, his toy got broken in the fight."

Brandon brightened. He had a plan to fix *that* part, at least. But before he could explain, his dad kept talking.

"I had to leave work early yesterday, Brandon. You know we can't afford for me to miss any hours. Things are tight enough as they are."

Brandon nodded and stared out the train window. That was why he was going into work with his dad this morning—Brandon's father couldn't take a sick day, and there was nobody else to stay home and watch him.

The Q train rattled up onto the Manhattan Bridge, and Brandon saw the World Trade Center in the distance. It was hard to miss. The gray, rectangular Twin Towers stood more than twice as tall as the other skyscrapers around them at the southern end of Manhattan. The two towers were almost identical, except for the huge red-and-white antenna on the roof of the North

Tower. That was where Brandon's dad worked. He was a kitchen manager at a restaurant called Windows on the World at the very top of the North Tower, on the 107th floor.

"Brandon, what do we say about us? About you and me?" his dad asked.

Brandon gave the answer that had been drilled into him since his mother had died from cancer five years ago, when he was only four. "We're a team," he said.

"*We're a team,*" his dad repeated. "That's what we've always said. This is how we survive, right? *Together.* It's you and me against the world. But you shut me out on this one. And you let down the team."

The disappointment in his father's voice was like a punch in the gut, and Brandon felt tears come to his eyes. It hurt way worse than if his dad had just been mad at him.

The train went underground again, and the bright blue sky disappeared.

After a quick transfer to the R train, Brandon and his dad got off at their stop. They climbed the subway stairs into the underground mall below the World Trade Center Plaza. The mall was already packed by eight fifteen a.m., with long breakfast lines at Au Bon Pain and the Coffee Station.

Brandon trailed along behind his dad, lost in his thought. He wished he could have a do-over. Go back in time and make a different decision. But even if he *could* go back, what would he do differently? Stuart Pendleton *deserved* to get punched in the nose.

"I still don't think I should have been suspended," Brandon told his dad as they cut through the bustling crowd. Five subway lines and the PATH train from New Jersey all stopped at stations below the mall, and three different exits led up to Manhattan streets.

"So you think you just get to go around punching people you don't like?" his dad asked.

"If they're bullies, yes!" Brandon said. They turned left at the Warner Bros. store, with its big statues of Daffy Duck and Bugs Bunny, but he hardly noticed them today.

"There are rules, Brandon," his dad said as they headed for the escalators at the far end of the mall. "You punch somebody, you get suspended, no matter why you did it. Your actions have to have consequences. If they didn't, *you'd* be the bully."

Brandon couldn't believe what he was hearing. *Him?* A bully?

"That's what a bully is," his dad said. "Somebody who pushes people around and never gets in trouble for it."

Brandon frowned as he and his dad got on the escalator. *He* wasn't the bully here! Stuart Pendleton was the bully!

Brandon suddenly remembered his plan—the one for making things right with Cedric. They hadn't passed the Sam Goody store, but Brandon knew there was one here in the mall. He closed his eyes and went through the layout in his head. *Back down to the J.Crew store, then right, past the Hallmark store and the Bath and Body Works.* Yes. That's where the Sam Goody was, with its CDs and DVDs and toys.

Toys like the Wolverine claws he'd broken.

Brandon patted the wad of dollars and change he'd stuffed in the pocket of his jeans before leaving home. While his dad was working in the restaurant at the top of the tower, Brandon would come back downstairs, buy a pair of Wolverine claws for Cedric, and—

"Whoa! Look out!"

Brandon turned. A Black man in a double-breasted suit with a shaved head and a beard stood behind them on the escalator, trying to juggle a briefcase, a folded-up newspaper, and a cardboard drink holder carrying three steaming cups of coffee. He was about to drop at least one thing, if not everything, and the drooping drink holder looked like it was going to be the first to go.

Brandon caught the edge of the cardboard tray before it toppled over, and his dad quickly grabbed hold of the briefcase.

"Whew. Thank you," the businessman said. "That almost turned into a very bad day for all of us."

Brandon and his dad helped the man rearrange his things, and they parted ways at the top of the escalator, in the lobby of the North Tower of the World Trade Center. Brandon stood for a second and stared. He'd been here many times before, but the size of the place always surprised him.

The lobby was as wide as four tractor trailers parked end to end, and so tall you could stack them three high and still not hit the ceiling. Up above, there was a wrap-around mezzanine where a second floor would have been, leaving the space open and airy. Sunlight bounced off the windows of the smaller buildings across the street and made the North Tower's lobby glow.

Brandon's dad led him toward the reception desk, passing men and women of all colors and sizes wearing suits and dresses and delivery uniforms and casual clothes. Brandon's dad had once told him that more than twenty-five thousand people worked in the North Tower alone. Most of those people weren't here yet, but the lobby was still crowded.

A security guard took Brandon's picture for his temporary ID badge, and Brandon waited for the machine to spit it out.

"I took him to the nurse's station," Brandon said.

His dad frowned down at him. "Took who to what nurse's station?"

"Stuart Pendleton," Brandon said. "The boy I hit."

Brandon wanted his dad to understand he wasn't a bully. That he wasn't some mean kid who went around punching other people without feeling bad about it.

"Once I saw his nose was bleeding, I helped him up and took him to the nurse's station."

Brandon's dad sighed. "That's nice, Brandon. But did you ever stop to think that maybe you shouldn't have given the boy a bloody nose to begin with?"

"Here you go, kid," the security guard said, handing Brandon his temporary ID card.

Brandon stared at the picture of himself. Dark, messy hair. Brown skin and high cheekbones, like his dad. A slightly upturned nose and blue eyes, like his mom. His name—*Brandon Chavez*—was printed beneath the picture, along with the date:

September 11, 2001.

"Come on," said Brandon's dad. "Let's go upstairs."

RESHMINA

RIGHT HERE, RIGHT NOW

"Five. Six. Seven. Eight." Reshmina counted in English as she picked up sticks for firewood. "Nine. Eleven." No—she had missed a number. Ten.

Reshmina stood and straightened her back. It was early morning, crisp and cool. The sky was a brilliant, cloudless blue, and Reshmina could see all the way to the towering mountain range that separated her home in Afghanistan from its neighboring country, Pakistan. The mountains were arid and brown, with snowcapped peaks. Down below, a green-and-gold patchwork of rice paddies and wheat fields and vegetable gardens lined a lazy brown river.

It was September. Soon, Reshmina realized with a pang of sadness, it would be time for the harvest. Reshmina's parents would keep her home from school to help. Reshmina hated missing school.

"Taliban attack!" her twin brother, Pasoon, cried, leaping out from behind the bush where he'd been hiding.

Reshmina screamed in surprise, and the stack of firewood in her arms went flying.

Pasoon held a stick like a rifle and pretended to shoot at her. "Pakow pakow pakow!"

Reshmina shoved her brother with both hands. "Pasoon, you snake! Look what you made me do! Now I have to start all over."

Pasoon cackled at his own joke. "I was just trying to help. See?" He offered her his fake rifle. "I brought you a stick."

Reshmina snatched the stick from him. "Some help," she said. "How long were you waiting behind that bush?"

"All morning!" Pasoon said, pleased with himself. "You took forever to get here."

Reshmina and Pasoon were both thin, with round faces, brown skin, big brown eyes, and black hair. Pasoon's hair was short and unkempt while Reshmina's was long, carefully combed, and tucked under a black headscarf. Pasoon was a little taller than Reshmina, but they looked more alike than different.

How they *lived* was another matter entirely.

As a boy, Pasoon had time for games and practical jokes. His only chore was to take the goats up into the mountains to graze for a few hours. As a girl, Reshmina worked from the moment she woke up until she went to sleep at night. While Pasoon had been lying in wait for her, Reshmina had been hauling water up from the river. There were also clothes to be washed, rugs to be beaten and stacked, floors to be swept, animals to be fed, food to be cooked—*and*, every afternoon, the two-kilometer walk back and forth to school. Pasoon didn't even do *that* anymore. He'd quit going to school a year ago.

Pasoon bent down and began collecting some of the sticks he'd made Reshmina drop.

"I heard you practicing your English," he told her. Their native language was Pashto, the language of the Afghan mountains. They both knew some Dari too— the language spoken in much of the rest of Afghanistan. Of the two of them, only Reshmina had kept up with her English lessons.

"Why?" Pasoon asked.

"What do you mean why?"

"I mean why bother?" said Pasoon.

"I'm learning English because I'm going to be a teacher," Reshmina told him.

"*Be a teacher?*" Pasoon cried. "The man you marry is never going to let you work!"

Reshmina frowned. Pasoon was probably right. In Afghanistan, women had to do what their husbands told them to, and most men told their wives they had to stay home and take care of the house and raise a family.

Reshmina's schoolteacher was a woman, but she was from Australia and unmarried.

"I'll teach until I'm married, then," Reshmina said. But she knew that was a fantasy. Reshmina's parents had just arranged for her sister Marzia to be married to an older man when she turned sixteen next year. When Reshmina turned sixteen five years from now, she'd be married off too. She would go right from school to her new home.

Reshmina's parents had planned the same fate for Reshmina's eldest sister, Hila. But Hila had died before she could be married.

Reshmina felt a rush of sadness at the thought of her sister. Hila, who'd been like a second mother to Reshmina and Pasoon. Who'd made up stories for them, and taught them to read. Who loved jumping out and scaring them and chasing them all around the house pretending to be a mountain lion.

Reshmina fought off the pain of remembering.

"Besides," she said now, turning back to Pasoon, "it's 2019. Everyone speaks English."

Pasoon scoffed. "Darwesh and Amaan say that when the Taliban win and the Americans leave, nobody will care about speaking English anymore."

Reshmina shook her head. Darwesh and Amaan were two foolish boys who were three years older than Pasoon, and he followed them around like a baby chick. Darwesh and Amaan had left home last month, and everyone knew where they had gone. The same place all the young men went, eventually. Up into the mountains to join the Taliban.

Talib meant "student" in Pashto, and the Taliban had begun as a group of men who had studied at traditional Islamic schools. The Taliban followed a *very* strict interpretation of religious law, and during Afghanistan's last civil war in the 1990s, they'd fought their way to power.

Reshmina's mother and grandmother had told Reshmina horror stories about life under Taliban rule: how the Taliban beat men for not growing beards, massacred families, burned down schools, and put on public executions in the soccer stadium in Afghanistan's capital, Kabul. It had been even worse for women. The Taliban banned girls from going to school or having jobs, beat women who left their houses without a male family member, and sold girls into slavery. The American army had driven the Taliban out of power twenty years ago, but the Taliban were still around, hiding out in the mountains, right where Reshmina lived. And the American army was still here too, fighting the Taliban alongside the Afghan National Army.

The Taliban had changed though. They were far less organized now. Some of their fighters were still motivated by the Taliban's extreme interpretation of Islam.

Others welcomed any excuse to drive the foreign invaders from Afghanistan. Some of them were just poor boys from mountain villages who were hungry and needed a job. But they all shared a hatred of the Americans and the American-supported Afghan government, and fought them both whenever and however they could.

Pasoon turned his back to Reshmina to pick up another stick, and Reshmina saw her chance for revenge. She worked little sticks between the fingers of each hand like claws and snuck up on Pasoon.

"Snow leopard attack!" she cried, and jumped on his back.

Pasoon screamed and dropped all the sticks he'd been collecting. Reshmina scratched at his neck with her makeshift claws, and Pasoon fell to the ground. In seconds they were tumbling and wrestling and laughing like they had when they were little, before Hila had died and Marzia had been promised in marriage and Pasoon had started talking about joining the Taliban.

At last Pasoon swept her knees out from under her, and Reshmina fell to the dirt beside him. They lay on their backs, panting and staring up into the cloudless blue sky, and Reshmina's hand found Pasoon's. He didn't pull away, and Reshmina smiled. This, right here, right now, was what Reshmina wanted most in the world. What had been slipping away from her, bit by bit, as she and her brother got older. If only she could go back in time, to those days when she and Pasoon had chased each other in the hills and gone swimming in the deepest part of the river and played hide-and-seek in the caves beneath their village.

Reshmina wished she could capture this moment in a jar. Preserve it in amber. Hila was lost to her, and soon Marzia would be married and gone, and Pasoon would follow Darwesh and Amaan into the mountains, and Reshmina . . .

From their village around the mountain came the sudden sound of a woman's cry. Then Reshmina heard a man yell, "Open up!"

Reshmina felt goose bumps on her skin. Pasoon pulled his hand from hers, and they both sat up quickly. Something was happening in their village.

Something bad.

Pasoon hopped to his feet and ran down the hill, and Reshmina hurried to follow him. They rounded the mountain and slid to a stop at the edge of the river.

Afghan men wearing green camouflage uniforms and carrying automatic rifles—soldiers from the Afghan National Army—were pounding on doors in Reshmina's village, demanding to be let inside homes. And there were *American* soldiers with them, directing their movements.

Reshmina gasped. Her village was being raided!

BRANDON

WINDOWS ON THE WORLD

Brandon loved riding the express elevator that zipped up all one hundred and seven floors of the North Tower without stopping. It was a kind of magic—one minute you were on the ground, and the next you were more than *a thousand feet* up in the sky. Brandon watched with anticipation as the red digital numbers above the door flew by—101, 102, 103, 104, 105, 106—and then *ding!* They were there. The 107th floor. Windows on the World.

The restaurant took up the entire floor, and diners were already scattered at different tables for breakfast. Ms. Eng, the woman who managed the seating area, greeted Brandon as he entered, but he ran straight for the windows that gave the famous restaurant its name.

The sky was still brilliant blue and cloudless, and

Brandon could see far across the Hudson River, all the way into New Jersey. Huge container ships in the harbor looked like toy boats from up here. A news helicopter flew by *underneath him*. Brandon's skin tingled, and he felt dizzy as his brain struggled to reconcile standing so high up with being safe behind the glass. Every part of him seemed to be screaming, *"You. Can't. Possibly. Be. Up. This. High."* But he was, and for this brief, wonderful moment he felt like the king of the world. Or at least of New York and New Jersey.

"All right, Brandon. If you have to be here, I'm going to put you to work," his father called. "Take a water pitcher and fill the flower vases on all the empty tables."

Brandon rolled his eyes, but he didn't complain.

He started with the tables on the other side of the restaurant, where he could get a peek at more amazing views. Right next door was the gargantuan World Trade Center South Tower. It was the twin of the North Tower, except that it had an observation deck at the top instead of a restaurant, and no antenna. Its windows, like the North Tower's, were partially obscured by thin aluminum supports. Beyond the South Tower, far off in the distance, was the Statue of Liberty—from this height, just a speck on an island in New York Harbor.

Brandon finished filling the vases and headed for the eastern side of the restaurant, which offered picture-postcard views of the Brooklyn and Manhattan Bridges.

Brandon had been down there less than a half an hour ago, looking up at the Twin Towers from the Q train.

I think I can see my house from here, Brandon thought.

CRASH!

The loud noise from the other side of the restaurant made Brandon flinch. An alarm went off, and someone yelled, "Help! Fire!"

Diners stood from their tables, wondering what to do. Brandon set his pitcher down, suddenly afraid. The commotion was coming from the kitchen, where his dad was.

"I'm sure it's nothing," Ms. Eng told the diners. "No need to panic."

Brandon ran to the kitchen and stopped at the door. A great towering flame burned on one of the stovetops, licking at the ceiling. Brandon could feel the heat through his clothes. The kitchen floor was littered with broken dishes and food, and cooks and servers stood back from the fire in fear.

Brandon's dad was there, but he wasn't hurt. He wasn't afraid of the fire either.

"What are you all standing around for?" Brandon's dad said. He grabbed a towel and started to beat out the flames.

Brandon relaxed. He'd seen kitchen fires before. They were always spectacular, but ultimately not very dangerous. Grease would catch fire on a stove and burn hot and bright, and within half a minute someone would put it out by throwing a pot lid on top or smothering it with a towel.

Ordinarily, Brandon would have stayed to watch. But this, he realized, was the perfect distraction for him to slip away down to the underground mall and buy the replacement Wolverine gloves for Cedric. He patted his pocket again, feeling the lump of bills and coins. Getting the mess in the kitchen cleaned up would keep his dad busy for a while, and Brandon could be down to Sam Goody and back before his dad even knew he was gone.

Brandon hurried past Ms. Eng, who was still reassuring the diners, and over to the elevators. He pressed the DOWN button and looked over his shoulder nervously, hoping his dad wouldn't come out of the kitchen and see him.

Ding!

An elevator door opened. It wasn't the express elevator that went straight back down to the lobby. This one only went to the Sky Lobby on the 78th floor. From there, Brandon would have to take two more elevators to get downstairs. It wouldn't be as fast, but Brandon didn't want to wait around for someone to spot him.

Brandon jumped onto the elevator, just missing the closing doors.

He'd made it! Brandon leaned against the railing at the back of the elevator and smiled. He couldn't fix punching Stuart Pendleton in the nose, but he *could* fix breaking Cedric's Wolverine gloves, and that made him feel better.

The elevator slowed to a stop, and an elderly white man with silver hair got on. The elevator stopped again, and a blonde white woman in a purple pantsuit got on, followed by a big white guy in a blue blazer and red necktie.

I shouldn't have taken the local, Brandon thought. He glanced at his LEGO watch. 8:45 a.m. He was going to have to be speedy if he didn't want his dad to find out he was gone.

The elevator stopped *again*, and a man with brown skin and a graying beard wheeled a catering cart with empty dishes onto the elevator. He wore a light blue turban that matched the color of his Windows on the World uniform. Brandon froze. The man wore a name tag that said SHAVINDER. Brandon didn't recognize him, but he worried Shavinder might have seen Brandon around the restaurant and would know he was Leo Chavez's son. Brandon slipped farther behind the big white guy and watched the red digital numbers of the floors tick by. 94, 93, 92, 91, 90, 89, 88, 87, 86—

THOOM.

Something boomed above them, and the elevator suddenly went sideways.

Brandon grabbed on to the handrail to not fall over. Two other passengers—the blonde woman and the old man—*did* fall down, but Brandon couldn't have helped them even if he'd tried. The elevator was shuddering so wildly it felt like someone had taken him by the shoulders and was shaking the life out of him.

And then a new sensation: They were falling! No— the elevator car wasn't falling—it was *leaning*. Farther and farther and farther to the side, like they were on the Tilt-a-Whirl at Coney Island. Brandon held tight on to the handrail, digging in his heels, while the other passengers slid forward until they were all pinned to the opposite wall. The serving cart toppled over, spilling dishes and water and silverware.

Brandon's mind raced, trying to make sense of what was happening. The elevator couldn't swing this far in the elevator shaft. Elevator shafts were just a little bigger than the elevators inside them. That meant—*that meant the whole tower was leaning*. All one hundred and seven floors. That wasn't possible, was it?

The elevator stopped tilting, and Brandon held his breath. No one uttered a word. Then slowly, sickeningly, popping and complaining the whole way, the elevator began to right itself. It came up straight and Brandon caught his breath, but then the elevator swayed in the *other* direction. The passengers who'd been pinned to the wall scrambled to cling to the railing to stay put. Brandon closed his eyes and braced himself as silverware and broken plates came skittering across the floor toward him.

But the elevator didn't swing so far this time. It shuddered and groaned its way back upright. The lights flickered but stayed on, and suddenly everything was quiet again.

"What the *hell*—?" the silver-haired man started to say.

And then the elevator began to slide.

RESHMINA

A CLEAN SLATE

Reshmina and her brother ran up the steps of their village, Reshmina's thoughts racing faster than her feet.

Americans were here.

Reshmina had encountered Afghan National Army soldiers before—they had a base nearby and checked in occasionally with the village elders. The Americans were a different story. Reshmina had seen their helicopters flying over the valley, heard the pops and booms from their far-off gunfights with the Taliban. But in her eleven years, the Americans hadn't once come to her remote little village. Why were they here now?

Like most other villages in the province, Reshmina's was built into the side of a mountain. Flatland for farming was scarce, so houses were stacked one on top of the other, like a pyramid of square pieces of sweet bread.

To get from the bottom to their house near the top, Reshmina and her brother had to climb a long set of switchback stairs cut into the rock.

Reshmina and Pasoon turned a corner and saw a group of ANA soldiers just ahead. They looked very young—almost like teenagers. *Boy-men*, Reshmina thought. Like Darwesh and Amaan, Pasoon's friends.

Two of the soldiers held an old man named Ezatullah outside his home while other soldiers went inside.

"They're searching all the houses," Reshmina whispered. But what were they looking for?

Ezatullah started to argue with the soldiers, and Pasoon took Reshmina by the hand and pulled her along past them, up the stairs.

At the house just below theirs, Reshmina saw an American soldier giving instructions to a team of Afghan soldiers. The American's uniform was sand-colored, unlike the green camouflage the ANA soldiers wore. He had more equipment too—and a bigger gun.

Reshmina pulled her headscarf over her face and looked away as she and Pasoon slipped by.

"Did you see that?" Pasoon hissed. "Afghans taking orders from an American in our own country!"

They came at last to their house, a squat square home made of mud and brick and wood. Pasoon threw open the door, and Reshmina followed him inside.

There were only three rooms in their house—a front

room where the family ate their meals, a room beyond that where the women spent most of their time and where the family slept, and their tiny kitchen in the back with its cooking pit. Each room had a dirt floor with rugs on it but no other furniture.

Reshmina ran to the women's room. Her older sister Marzia sat on the floor picking the bad bits out of a bowl of uncooked rice, and their *anaa*—their grandmother—did needlework and sang softly to Reshmina's little brother, Zahir, who rolled around on a rug beside her. Marzia looked pretty in her pink dress and teal headscarf. Anaa wore a blue-and-white flower-print dress and a blue shawl.

"The Afghan army is here!" Reshmina cried. "They're searching everyone's homes!"

Marzia stood. "What? Why?"

"It's the Americans. They're the ones in charge," Pasoon said. "They don't need a reason!"

Reshmina's father came into the room on his wooden crutch. The rugged mountains of southern Afghanistan had stolen years from their *baba*, carving the lines and wrinkles of an older man into his reddish-brown face. His beard was short and bushy, more gray now than black, and he wore baggy pants, a long olive-green tunic, and a gray turban.

Someone pounded on their door. *Boom boom boom!*

Reshmina's *mor*—her mother—hurried out of the

kitchen. Mor was clutching a gray scarf around her face. "What is it? Who's come?" she asked.

"The army," Baba told her. "I will speak to them."

Pasoon followed Baba to the front door while Reshmina waited nervously with the rest of her family in the women's room. A few minutes later, Reshmina heard the soldiers enter her home and begin to search the family room. She could tell that Baba had come inside with them but not Pasoon.

Reshmina couldn't make herself stop shaking. What did the soldiers want? She and her family had nothing to hide! Marzia took her hand and squeezed it, and Reshmina knew her older sister was frightened too.

Baba led the Afghan soldiers into the women's room. The American soldier Reshmina had passed on the stairs was with them. He had brown skin and was short, with wide shoulders.

"Baba, where is Pasoon?" Reshmina asked her father.

"They're keeping him outside," Baba said.

Anaa continued to do her needlework, unperturbed, but Reshmina's mother snatched up little Zahir, then pulled Reshmina and Marzia to her, like the soldiers had come to take them all away from her.

"Tell them we're not here to hurt them," the American soldier said in English. Despite her fear, Reshmina felt a small thrill go through her. Her English lessons had paid off. She understood what he said!

"The soldiers are not here to hurt you," someone said in Pashto, and Reshmina's jaw dropped as the translator stepped out from behind the American. The translator wore tan camouflage pants, tan body armor over a black long-sleeve shirt, and a green headscarf.

The translator was an Afghan woman!

"The Americans were told there is a cache of Taliban weapons in this village," the translator told Reshmina and her family in Pashto. "The Afghan National Army is here to search your house. The American sergeant is here as an advisor."

"There are no weapons here," Anaa said to the translator. "No Taliban either."

Reshmina was barely listening. All she could do was stare wide-eyed at the translator. All the Afghan women Reshmina knew were mothers, wives, and daughters. None of them had jobs outside the home—and especially not important jobs like translator, where they worked and talked with men outside their families.

"Who are you?" Reshmina whispered to the translator.

The woman smiled. "My name is Mariam. I'm from Kabul."

Reshmina couldn't believe it. It was like a whole new path had appeared before her that she hadn't known was there before. A whole new person she could become.

Mariam.

The two Afghan soldiers searched the women's room, and then the American soldier sent them to search the kitchen and the goat pens. The American certainly acted like he was in charge, just as Pasoon had said.

Reshmina studied the American again. This time she noticed a silly-looking stuffed animal tucked into the gear on his vest. The doll was all mouth and tongue and long spindly arms and legs, and it had a wild, mischievous look in its eyes. It was shabby and faded and dusty, like everything else in Afghanistan, and it was coming apart at one of the seams. Reshmina frowned. Why would the American be carrying something as strange as that? And what did it mean?

One of the Afghan soldiers came back into the room with a small object in his hand. Reshmina recognized it immediately—it was a toy airplane their sister Hila had bought Pasoon as a gift two years ago. Now that Hila was gone, that plane was Pasoon's most treasured possession in the world.

"I found this in a hole, high up on the back wall of the house," the soldier said in Pashto to Mariam, who translated for the American soldier.

The American took the toy and turned to Reshmina's family. "Why was this hidden?"

Mariam translated, and Anaa laughed. "It's my grandson's. He's a boy. He hides things."

Reshmina nodded. Anaa was right. Why should the soldiers care what Pasoon did with the little airplane? It was none of their business!

"It's only a toy," Baba told the Afghan soldier.

The American frowned and handed the airplane to Baba. "Tell them not to hide things from us," he told Mariam in English. "It makes them look suspicious."

The soldiers finished searching the house, and Baba escorted them and the American and Mariam back to the front door. Reshmina pulled away from her mother and followed them. Mor hissed, but Reshmina ignored her. She wanted to watch Mariam. Hear her.

Mariam and the American soldier stopped outside the house to speak to Baba. Reshmina saw that Pasoon was there too, flanked by two other ANA soldiers. Pasoon was scowling. His fists were clenched tight, and his arms were straight down at his sides. Reshmina could tell he was ready to fight.

"The sergeant says that he appreciates your cooperation," Mariam said to Baba and Pasoon, gesturing to the American. "He hopes we can put the past behind us and start over with a clean slate."

"*A clean slate?*" Baba asked. "When they force their way into our homes? When they kill our people?"

"They killed my sister Hila!" Pasoon cried, glaring at the American. He turned to the Afghan soldiers.

"And now you betray our country by working for them!" he snapped.

Reshmina's father put a hand on Pasoon's shoulder to calm him, but Pasoon shook him off

"This 'past' they speak of is our present," Baba told Mariam. "Are we supposed to forget about our mothers and fathers, our sons and daughters, our brothers and sisters the Americans have killed in their attacks? If someone came along and killed a village of *their* people, would they say, 'Ah well, time to start over with a clean slate'? Or would they swear revenge and promise never to forget?"

Reshmina wanted to cry. She hated the idea of revenge, but she too could never forget how the Americans had killed her sister. Sometimes she wished *they* could hurt as much as she did, just so they'd understand.

Mariam translated everything for the American soldier, expressing all their sorrow and frustration in English.

"Tell them not to let the Taliban into their village, and we'll leave them alone," the American said.

"Not let the Taliban in?" Reshmina cried in English, not waiting for Mariam to translate into Pashto. Baba and Pasoon couldn't understand her words, but they looked surprised that she was speaking up. "How can we stop the Taliban when you won't let us have weapons?" Reshmina asked.

"You always have a choice," the American told her. "You can pick our side, or their side."

"That's no choice at all," Mariam told the sergeant. "If these villagers side with the Americans, the Taliban will kill them. And if they side with the Taliban, you and the ANA will kill them. You're telling them to choose death!"

"I'm sorry," the sergeant said with a shrug. He moved on to the next house up the stairs, and the ANA soldiers followed him.

Mariam took a deep breath and looked at Reshmina. "I'm sorry too," she said, and she left to join the soldiers.

"What was all that about?" Pasoon asked Reshmina. The last part of the conversation had all been in English.

"Nothing," Reshmina said. Telling him would just make him angrier.

"I *hate* them," Pasoon said, and he spat on the ground.

Baba went back inside the house, and Reshmina started up the stairs.

"Wait—where are you going?" Pasoon asked her.

"I'm following that translator," Reshmina said.

"No, you can't!" said Pasoon. He grabbed her arm and glanced over his shoulder.

"Pasoon, what are you doing?" Her brother was suddenly acting very strange.

"Nothing," he said. "You just need to get your chores done. Come on. I'll help you sweep the floor."

Now Reshmina *knew* something was up. Pasoon never offered to help with her chores. She pulled herself free.

"Pasoon, what's going on?"

Pasoon looked around warily, then pulled Reshmina into a shadow on the stairs.

"It's the Taliban," he whispered. "*They* started the rumor there were weapons in our village, to lure the soldiers here. Darwesh and Amaan told me yesterday. It's a trap, Reshmina—the Taliban are going to attack the soldiers on their way out of the village!"

BRANDON

TRAPPED

The elevator kept sliding down—and not the way it was built to. Brandon could feel how wrong it was in the pit of his stomach. From the horrified looks on their faces, the other passengers in the elevator felt it too.

"Hit the emergency stop button," the blonde woman said.

Nobody moved. The elevator kept sliding. Above them, something groaned sickeningly.

"Hit the emergency stop!" the woman cried.

There was a loud *chung!* above them, and the floor of the car dropped like a stone. Brandon's heart jumped into his throat, and he lunged for the control panel and slapped the red STOP button. The elevator's emergency brakes grabbed hold with a squeal and the car jolted to a stop. Everyone tumbled to the ground, and then they were still.

Brandon's breath came fast and hard, and he panted with fear. What had just *happened*?

Something smelled like it was burning, but not like a kitchen fire. It had a chemical tinge to it, like when you squirted lighter fluid on the burning charcoal in a grill.

The passengers stirred and helped each other to their feet. Brandon's legs were trembling so much he almost couldn't stand.

"What the heck just happened?" the big man in the blue blazer asked.

None of them had an answer.

"I rode out Hurricane Belle in this tower in '76," said Shavinder, the Windows on the World worker. "During the hurricane, the towers swayed back and forth five yards each way. But it was nothing like *that*."

The silver-haired man clutched at the buttons on his shirt. "Good God, if this thing fell over, it'd reach all the way to Chinatown."

Brandon blanched. *The Twin Towers fall over?*

"That's not helping," the woman said. "Try the phone."

There was an emergency phone behind a metal panel, and Shavinder pressed the call button and waited.

"Yes! Hello!" he said after a moment, and Brandon

relaxed. If somebody knew they were in the elevator, they could come rescue them. "Yes, something happened, and we're stuck in an elevator around the 85th floor."

Brandon heard a calm voice on the other end answering back.

"He says there is some kind of problem on the 91st floor," Shavinder told the other passengers. "An explosion or something. He says— Hello? Hello, are you there? He's gone."

An explosion? Brandon thought. What could have exploded?

The big man took the phone from Shavinder and pressed the call button again. He shook his head. "The line's dead."

Black smoke crept through the seams at the top of the elevator, and Brandon felt a bead of sweat roll down his back. *Smoke?* Was there a fire? It was getting really hot too.

"We've got to get out of here!" the silver-haired man cried.

"Stay cool," the woman told him. She dug a cell phone out of her briefcase and flipped it open, but she couldn't get a signal. Nobody else had a cell phone to try.

They were trapped and cut off from the rest of the world.

Brandon put his head in his hands and tried not to cry. He was scared and separated from the person he relied on the most—his dad.

It's you and me against the world, Brandon. This is how we survive.

But how was Brandon supposed to survive without him?

Smoke tickled the back of Brandon's throat, and he coughed. The old man coughed too, longer and harder. Brandon could now *see* the black smoke among them, curling and twisting like something alive.

The big man pulled cloth napkins from the wreckage of the cart. "Here, wrap these around your faces," he said.

"Dab them in some water first," Shavinder said. The overturned pitcher had a little water left in it, and he wet the napkins and handed them out. Brandon tied his napkin around his mouth and took a deep breath. It was still hard to breathe, but the napkin filtered out a lot of smoke. The old man kept coughing though, even with the damp napkin to help.

They all sat down on the floor to get as far away from the smoke as they could and went around introducing themselves. The blonde woman's name was Marni, and she was a stockbroker from Connecticut. Shavinder was born in New Delhi, India, and lived in Queens. He had worked at Windows on the World since it opened in

1976. The old man's name was Stephen. He was an investment banker who worked on the 101st floor and lived on the Upper West Side of Manhattan. He'd been a New Yorker all his life. The big man's name was Mike, and he lived in New Jersey. He was in the tower to interview for an insurance job.

"I'm Brandon," Brandon said when it was his turn. It was weird, talking to a bunch of grown-ups like he was one of them. But in a way, he was. It didn't matter whether they were young or old, or where they were from. They were all stuck in the same bad situation together.

"Wait, you're Leo Chavez's kid, aren't you?" Shavinder said. Brandon nodded. There was no sense hiding it now. Getting in trouble with his father was the least of his worries.

"Whaddya think that sound was?" Mike asked. "That snapping sound right before the kid hit the stop button? You think that was the elevator cable?"

Nobody answered him. So far no one seemed to be outright panicking, but Brandon realized he was shaking and he couldn't make himself stop.

He wished he could reach his dad. *If only I hadn't gone off on my own*, Brandon thought. *And all for some stupid Wolverine gloves.* What a fool he had been, and now he was going to choke to death inside this metal coffin.

"Kid, you with us?"

It was Mike. He and the others were looking at Brandon like they'd asked him something when he wasn't listening.

"We're gonna try to get out of here," Mike told him. "Can I lift you up so you can try the ceiling?"

Brandon agreed, and Mike boosted him up onto his shoulders. The smoke was heavier up there, and Brandon held his breath. He pushed and pounded on every inch of the ceiling, but nothing budged.

"Let's see if we can get the doors open instead," Shavinder said. He and Mike put their palms flat on the shiny metal doors of the elevator and pulled, and the doors opened a crack. Brandon felt a tiny thrill—maybe they were going to get out of here after all! He and Marni jumped in to help. Together the four of them pulled the elevator doors wide, and Shavinder jammed a metal serving tray between the doors to keep them open.

Brandon stepped back, expecting to see a hallway. Or at least part of one. Instead there was nothing but an unpainted gray wall, with the number *85* handwritten on it in pencil.

They were at the 85th floor, but they couldn't exit onto it.

Of course, Brandon realized. *The local becomes an express after the 97th floor.* There were no exits from this elevator until the Sky Lobby far below them on the 78th floor.

Which meant they really *were* trapped. And the smoke and heat were getting worse.

"It's drywall," Mike said. "Sheetrock. The stuff they make walls out of."

"Maybe we can bust our way out of here," said Marni.

Mike lifted a big foot and kicked at the wall.

THWACK!

Brandon leaned in close to look. All the kick had done was leave a footprint.

Mike waved everybody back, lowered his shoulder, and ran full tilt at the wall.

THUNK.

Nothing happened to the wall, but the elevator shuddered and jerked down another half a foot. Brandon thought he was going to have a heart attack.

"Let's not do *that* again!" Stephen said.

"Well, excuse me for trying to save our lives!" Mike snapped.

Everybody started yelling at each other, and Stephen started coughing again and couldn't stop. The smoke was getting worse, and now the elevator felt like a sauna.

Brandon plucked a butter knife out of the wreckage from the serving cart and held it up triumphantly. "What about this?" he cried.

Everybody stopped arguing and stared.

"Yeah, that's good. That could work!" Mike said, and Brandon felt a small flush of pride. Mike took the knife and hacked at the Sheetrock. A tiny bit of drywall crumbled into dust and rained down on the carpet, leaving a divot in the wall.

"There we go!" Mike said. He pulled off his blazer and loosened his tie, and went back to hacking on the wall. Shavinder grabbed a spatula-like serving utensil from the floor, and he used that on the hole too, taking turns with Mike. When they got tired, Marni and Brandon took turns. It was exhausting work. They didn't ask Stephen to help though, and he didn't offer. He was having enough trouble breathing already.

Smoke streamed in through every crack and every seam now, and something up above them popped and groaned.

Stephen tried the elevator phone again, but there was no answer.

What was going on? Where was everybody?

"We're all going to die here," Stephen wheezed.

"We're not going to die," Marni said, but it didn't sound like she believed it.

Brandon's arms shook, and he could barely aim straight when he whacked at the hole. How could he be trapped without his dad? Just this morning they had been together in another elevator. Why hadn't this happened then, when they could have helped each other?

Mike and Shavinder took over again, steadily chipping away at the wall. There wasn't *one* layer of drywall, they discovered, there were *three*. But working together, the elevator passengers managed to carve, yank, and kick a pizza-sized hole in the wall.

None of them could fit through it though—except for Brandon.

"Go, young man, go!" Shavinder told him.

"But we don't even know where it leads!" said Brandon. The space beyond the hole was dark and empty.

"Who cares, as long as it's not in here?" said Marni.

Brandon couldn't argue with that. He took a deep breath of wet, smoky air, and with Mike and Shavinder's help, he climbed up and out, into the unknown.

RESHMINA

PASHTUNWALI

Reshmina stared at her brother in horror. He *knew* the Taliban planned to attack? Did other people in the village know?

"Pasoon, the ANA are Afghans! Our own people! And I have no more love for the Americans than you do," she went on before her brother could speak, "but this betrayal will only make things worse for our village. The Americans will blame *us* for the attack."

"The Afghan soldiers made their choice when they agreed to do the Americans' dirty work for them," Pasoon said. "Besides, it's not like *we're* the ones carrying out the attack."

"No, we're just the ones not telling anyone about it," Reshmina said. "And if you won't, I will!"

"No! You can't!" Pasoon said. He grabbed for her

again, but Reshmina was too quick. She broke free and ran up the steps, Pasoon close on her heels.

Pop-pop! Pakoom. Pakoom.

The familiar sounds of gunfire and explosions made Reshmina duck and pull up short, her heart racing.

"It's started already!" Pasoon cried. Reshmina heard shouting and saw ANA soldiers scrambling down the steps for cover.

Pasoon grabbed Reshmina's hand and pulled her back toward their house. "Run, Reshmina!"

Reshmina raced back down the stairs and into their home, where her family was gathering in the front room. Baba wasn't there, and Reshmina realized Pasoon hadn't come inside with her.

THOOM. The ground rocked from a nearby explosion, and dirt rained down from the ceiling.

"It's safer in the back," Anaa said, leading them into the women's room. Mor disappeared into the kitchen.

PAK! PAK! PAK!

Gunfire erupted close enough nearby to rattle the dishes, and Reshmina and Marzia huddled together against the wall. Anaa pulled Zahir into her lap to sing to him, but the shooting and explosions didn't seem to bother the baby. He was already used to it. Reshmina didn't know if she would ever stop flinching at the sounds.

The earth shook again, and Marzia squeezed Reshmina's arm.

Dear God, please keep Baba and Pasoon safe out there, Reshmina prayed. *And Mariam*, she added, remembering the translator.

Even as the fighting continued outside, Reshmina found herself wondering what it would be like to go to Kabul someday and study to become a translator. She might be able to work for the Americans, like Mariam did. That had to pay well and would be worth more to her parents than bartering her off as a bride. Reshmina could put her English skills to work and support her entire family. It was an almost-impossible dream, but if Mariam could do it, so could Reshmina.

And without a dream, without ambition, what point was there to living?

Rifles and rockets boomed outside. Reshmina slid away from Marzia and pulled her blue English notebook from between the sleeping mats stacked in the corner. If becoming a translator was her way out, she wouldn't waste a second when she could be studying.

Reshmina's mother came into the room carrying a broom. "Oh no, none of that now," she said, spying Reshmina's notebook. She snatched it away and put the broom in Reshmina's hands. "You focus on your housework, not your schoolwork. And you get back to sorting that rice," she told Marzia. "Keep your heads down and learn how to be good wives. That's how a woman survives."

Mor left for the kitchen again, and Reshmina threw the broom down in frustration.

"Forgive your mother, Mina-jan," her grandmother told her. Zahir had fallen asleep in her lap, and Anaa took up her needlework again while Marzia returned to the rice.

"*Why?*" asked Reshmina. "All she wants is for me to learn how to be a good wife and marry a successful man. She has no dreams in her heart. No hope for something more!"

"You must understand, Mina-jan," Anaa said. "Your mother has never been allowed to dream. Me, I was born in Kabul long before the Americans came, or the Taliban. Before the Soviet invasion even. It was a golden time in Afghanistan," Anaa continued dreamily. "Women went to school and got jobs. One of my sisters became the principal of a school. Another woman I knew became a poet. We dressed differently too, like they do in Europe and America. I once wore a skirt that didn't even reach my knees. They called it a miniskirt."

"*Outside?*" Reshmina asked. She shared an astonished look with Marzia. Reshmina couldn't imagine wearing such a thing *in* the house, let alone *out*.

"Oh yes," their anaa said, laughing. "The boys rather liked it. And I did too."

Marzia blushed, and Reshmina got up and started

sweeping. The sounds of fighting still filtered in from outside.

"Some women wore the *chador*, but only if they wanted to," Anaa told them. A chador was a robe that covered a woman from head to toe, with only her face visible. "We were all Muslims, but in those days no one tried to force their beliefs on anyone else. There was real tolerance of others. We were brothers and sisters, working toward a better future. A better Afghanistan." Her face fell. "Then, forty years ago, the Russians invaded, and I fled to the mountains with your grandfather, God shower blessings on his grave." Anaa closed her eyes. "Afghanistan has known nothing but war ever since. *That* is the world your mother was born into."

"But so were we," Reshmina said, glancing at Marzia and Zahir.

As if to prove it, there came the *thump thump thump* of an American helicopter, and an even louder *BOOM* that made Reshmina flinch.

Anaa shook her head.

"When your mother was six, her father was killed by a missile while he was praying in his backyard," she said softly. "When she was your age, her older brother was killed by the Taliban for no reason that has ever been explained to her. Her husband—your father and my son—had his leg mangled by an old Soviet mine right after they were married. Two of her children died before they reached their fifth birthday, and her eldest daughter, your sister Hila, was killed by an American bomb."

Anaa closed her eyes again and sighed. She wore her sadness like a chador.

Reshmina swallowed. She knew about her sister and her father, of course, but her mother had never spoken about the rest.

"Is it any wonder your mother wishes only for you to be a good wife and married to a good husband?" Anaa asked Reshmina. "She has never known a better Afghanistan, as I have, and cannot trust in the promise of a brighter Afghanistan, as you do. She expects your life will be just as hard as hers, and she would protect you from anything so dangerous and painful as hope."

Reshmina suddenly felt sorry for her mother. Not only because of all the awful things she had lived through, but because she had never had anybody in her youth like Anaa or Reshmina's teacher—or even Mariam—to show her things could be better.

"When you're done sweeping, you can get back to gathering firewood, which you still haven't finished," Reshmina's mother said, making her jump. Mor had come back into the room while Reshmina was lost in thought. "They're done with their shooting," Mor said. "For now."

Reshmina realized her mother was right—there were no more shots or explosions. The battle was over.

"Yes, Mor," Reshmina said meekly.

I will try to be nicer to my mother in the future, she thought. *But I will not give up on my dreams.*

When Mor was gone, Reshmina picked up her English notebook and tucked it under her tunic before ducking out the back door to go collect firewood. As she made her way around the mountain, she read her English lessons aloud.

"Palwasha uses a computer to write an email. She talks to her friends on Facebook."

Reshmina had never used a computer, but she knew what one looked like. Some of the older girls at school practiced for when they would finally get a computer by tapping letters drawn on a piece of cardboard and reading books about the Windows operating system. Reshmina didn't know what Facebook was, but apparently it was very important.

Reshmina picked up a dry twig. "There is a party on the beach," she read aloud from her notebook. "Palwasha drives her mother to the party in her car."

"Nnnnnnnn," someone groaned.

Reshmina froze and looked around for the source of the sound. A few meters away, lying on his stomach among dried leaves and dirt, was an American soldier. His face was charred like a scorched pot, and there were dark, wet spots on his uniform. *Blood*, Reshmina realized. He must have been injured in the battle.

The soldier groaned again and dragged himself forward. Where was he going? He twisted his head this way and that, as though he was looking for something, but there were only scrub trees as far as Reshmina could see.

The soldier's head turned toward Reshmina, and she held her breath—but his eyes swept past her like he hadn't even seen her.

He's lost his eyesight, Reshmina realized. The black marks on his face—he had been wounded and couldn't see. If someone didn't help him, he would die out here in these woods. Or the Taliban would find him, and his death would be far more painful.

Reshmina frowned. Why should she care? The Americans had killed her sister, after all. *Pashtunwali*, the way of the Pashtun people, said that it was right and just to seek revenge against someone who had done you wrong. In Pashto, that revenge was called *badal*, and it never ran out. Reshmina could wait a dozen years—a *thousand*—and still take her revenge on someone who had wronged her.

Why not just slip away, then, and let this man die?

Reshmina flipped her notebook shut to leave, but she fumbled it. Her notebook hit the ground with a *flump*, and the soldier's head turned in her direction again.

"Is someone there?" he asked in English. "Hello? I

can't see, and my ears are ringing. I'm hurt. Hello? Can you help me? Please?"

Reshmina silently cursed her clumsiness. If she had been able to slip away without him hearing, she could have left the soldier to die and been done with it. But now he had heard her and had specifically asked her for help. Just as Pashtunwali gave her the right to revenge, it also said that when a person asked for help or protection, no Pashtun could refuse—no matter who was asking, friend or foe. That was *nanawatai*. What the Americans would call "refuge."

Reshmina sagged. She could still slip away and have her revenge, but now it would mean denying aid to someone who had asked for it.

"Hello?" the American soldier asked again, his voice weak. "Please," he begged. "Whoever you are, will you help me?"

BRANDON

IN CASE OF EMERGENCY

A motion sensor picked up Brandon climbing out of the hole in the wall, and fluorescent lights in the ceiling flickered on.

He had landed in the middle of a bathroom. A *ladies'* bathroom. But Brandon didn't have time to be embarrassed. He scrambled to his feet and peered back through the hole at the people still trapped in the elevator.

"I'll bring help!" he promised, and ran for the bathroom door.

Brandon burst out into a corridor. He ran past a fire extinguisher and fire hose box hanging on the wall and into the first office he came to—a company with the name HYAKUGO BANK printed on the door. He saw a reception desk and a couple of chairs for visitors, but no one was around.

"Hello?" Brandon called. There was no smoke here. He pulled down the wet napkin he'd tied around his face and took a deep breath of fresh air. "Is anybody here? We need help!"

Brandon ran past the reception desk. A small group of people stood together at the far wall, staring out the window at something.

"Hey!" Brandon said, running toward them. "Hey, we need—"

Brandon stopped short, mesmerized by what he saw out the window.

Paper. The sky was filled with thousands and thousands of sheets of paper, flipping and falling like the ticker tape parade when the Yankees had won the World Series last year. But this wasn't right. No one could have thrown these papers out a window on purpose. The World Trade Center windows didn't *open*.

Large chunks of glass and metal sliced through the paper blizzard, and some kind of liquid poured down the side of the building, even though it wasn't raining.

Brandon's stomach twisted. Something very bad had happened above them in the North Tower. But what? And how high up? All the way up at Windows on the World? Was Brandon's dad all right?

"Gas explosion," one of the bankers said. "Has to be."

"No way," said another banker. "The World Trade Center doesn't have gas lines in it."

"Please, we need help," Brandon cut in, making them jump. "Four people. Trapped in an elevator. There's a lot of smoke—"

"Where, kid?" a man asked.

"I'll show you!"

Two men and one woman from the group followed Brandon back down the hall and into the bathroom. Brandon was almost afraid to look through the hole. What if the elevator had fallen while he was gone? What if everyone inside was dead? Dark black smoke poured from the hole, making it hard to see, but Brandon heard Stephen cough, and he sagged with relief. His friends were still there!

"Oh my God," said one of the men who'd come with Brandon.

"Here, get back," the other banker said. The two men took turns kicking at the drywall, and the woman ran back to the office to call 911.

Brandon heard the elevator car drop suddenly. Dishes clattered, and everybody inside cried out in surprise and terror. The car jerked to a stop a foot lower, and Brandon held his breath. If the car dropped too much farther, the passengers wouldn't be able to reach the hole.

And if it fell down all the way . . .

"Hurry!" Brandon told the two men. "We have to get them out!"

The bankers were kicking at the drywall as hard and fast as they could, but they were already panting hard and sweating through their dress shirts. The smoke was getting worse too. Brandon coughed and looked around frantically. He had to *do* something. The help he'd brought wasn't enough, and they didn't have time to wait for building security or firemen.

Firemen, Brandon thought, and he had a sudden inspiration. He ran back out into the hall. There—the fire hose box! Brandon didn't want the hose curled up inside it. He wanted what was in *front* of the hose, right behind the glass.

A fire ax!

The instructions on the window said IN CASE OF EMERGENCY, BREAK GLASS. *Well*, thought Brandon, *if ever there was an emergency, this is it.* He yanked the fire extinguisher from its cradle and used the heavy thing like a battering ram.

Krissh!

The glass shattered, and Brandon cleared out the rest of the shards enough to reach inside. He grazed his wrist on a piece of glass and pulled his arm away with a hiss, but he'd be all right. He'd had worse injuries wiping out on his skateboard.

The important thing was, he had the ax.

Brandon ran back to the bathroom, where the two bankers were standing bent over, their hands on their knees. They were out of breath, and the smoke was even thicker than before.

"Look out!" Brandon cried. Shaking from panic and fear, Brandon lifted the big ax over his head and swung it down hard on the ragged break in the drywall.

Whack!

The ax knocked off a chunk of Sheetrock, but Brandon didn't hit it square on. The ax kicked away from the wall and slammed into the floor below the hole—*chank!*—shattering the bathroom's tiles.

"Whoa whoa whoa!" one of the bankers said, taking the ax from Brandon. "Good job, kid, but I got it from here."

Brandon stood back as the man swung the ax at the wall. He was stronger, and his aim was better. In less than a minute, he had opened up a hole big enough for Marni to squeeze through. When she could stand again, she wrapped Brandon in an I-can't-believe-we're-alive hug. Ordinarily, Brandon would have felt funny hugging a stranger, but now he hugged her back with relief.

Mike and Shavinder were able to help Stephen get through the hole next. He was still having trouble breathing, and Marni went to get him water. Finally Mike and Shavinder squeezed through the hole, and then everyone was out of the horrible elevator.

Shavinder gave Brandon a tight hug. "You saved us, Brandon," he said.

Brandon pointed to the men from the bank. "They did the work."

The banker with the ax wiped the sweat from his brow and smiled. "I guess chopping all that wood as a kid back in Wisconsin paid off," he said.

Marni tried her cell phone again, and this time she got a signal. She stepped to the corner of the bathroom with a finger to one ear and her phone to the other.

"Does anyone know what happened?" Shavinder asked the bankers.

"Felt like an earthquake to me," one of them replied.

"Yes, yes, I'm all right!" Marni told someone on the phone. "The signal's bad, hon, I can't . . . Yes, we were trapped in an elevator, but . . ." She was quiet for a moment. "Oh my God," she said. She turned to face the rest of them. "My husband says an airplane hit the building. A passenger jet. It's all over the news!"

"My God," Stephen said. "That must be why the building tilted! We were in the elevator when the plane hit."

A plane? Hit the building? Brandon felt a jolt go through him. That didn't make sense. How could you fly a plane into one of the Twin Towers by accident? They were the biggest, tallest buildings in the city, and there wasn't a cloud in the sky. No pilot in his right mind would—

Screeeeech!

Brandon heard the sound of metal grinding against metal, and he flinched. He and the others glanced back at the hole just in time to see the elevator car plummet down the shaft.

Nobody moved, and nobody spoke. Everyone was waiting and listening for the elevator car to hit bottom, but the crash never came.

Or maybe it was just so far down they couldn't hear it.

Brandon exhaled and slumped forward. Mike cursed underneath his breath, and Stephen let out a single sob. They had come *that close* to plummeting to their deaths.

"Hon? I'll call you back when I get out," Marni said into her phone, and flipped it closed.

In a daze, Brandon followed everyone out of the bathroom. The two bankers went back to their office, and the elevator survivors stood in a huddle.

"The plane must have hit somewhere high up," Mike said quietly. "Cut through the elevator cables."

"My dad!" Brandon said suddenly. "He's in Windows on the World! What if the plane hit the 107th floor?" He exchanged a frantic glance with Shavinder.

Stephen's eyes searched the ceiling. "My company is spread out over five floors. What if it hit one of those?"

Marni put a hand to her mouth. "My company covers

eight floors, right above us. And there were half a dozen people at work already this morning!"

"I'm sure they're all right," Mike said.

But there was no way he could know that, Brandon thought. There was no way any of them could know what floor the plane had hit.

One of the bankers came back from his office. "Claudia got 911 on the phone," he reported. "They said to stay put and wait for the firemen."

Mike shook his head. "Not me. I'm done. I think escaping that elevator deserves taking the rest of the day off."

The other elevator survivors nodded.

"I am *not* getting into another elevator. Maybe ever," Shavinder said. He gestured to the door that led to a stairwell. "It's eighty-five flights of stairs down, or twenty-two flights up."

"Up? Why would we go up if that's where the plane hit?" asked Mike.

"The stairs might still be clear, and they can take us off the roof in helicopters," Shavinder explained. "They did it once before, in '93. And it's a lot shorter trip."

"I left my purse and things in my office" said Marni.

"You can come back and get them tomorrow," Shavinder told her.

Stephen coughed. "I can't go up," he said. "I'm sorry. I'm still having trouble breathing."

"I'll help you go down, no worries," said Mike.

"So will I," Shavinder said.

Stephen nodded gratefully, and each man took one of Stephen's arms over their shoulders. Marni followed them. The bankers decided to stay.

Nobody asked Brandon what he wanted to do. Maybe they all just assumed he would go along with the group from the elevator. But when they entered the stairwell and everybody else started going down, Brandon knew he couldn't go with them. He kept hearing his dad's voice in his head.

Brandon, what do we say about us? About you and me?

"We're a team," Brandon said aloud. "That's how we survive. Together."

Brandon tied the wet napkin back around his face and started to climb the stairs up to Windows on the World.

RESHMINA

THE AMERICAN DEVIL

Reshmina took a deep breath and made her decision.

"I am here," she told the soldier in English. "I will go and bring my father to help you."

"No, wait," the soldier said. "Please. Don't leave me. I can't see." He reached out a hand.

Reshmina took a step back and shook her head, then remembered the soldier couldn't see her. "I cannot touch you," she told him. It was forbidden for a woman or girl to touch a man who wasn't related to her.

Anguish and frustration creased the soldier's face. "Right. Of course," he said, lowering his hand. He sniffed, fighting back tears.

Reshmina understood why the soldier was distraught. He was badly injured and alone. Reshmina was his only hope for survival, and if she left him now, he couldn't be sure she would return.

She had a thought. "I cannot touch you, and I cannot bring you back to my home without asking my father first," Reshmina said. "Instead, I will walk back to my home *very slowly—*"

"No, please," the soldier said again, cutting her off. "Don't leave me!"

Reshmina huffed. He wouldn't let her finish! "I will walk back to my home *very slowly*," Reshmina said again. "And I will practice my English out loud along the way. If somebody happens to *follow me*, there is nothing I can do to stop them."

Reshmina saw the soldier relax, then nod. "I understand," he whispered. "Thank you."

Reshmina turned around and began walking slowly back toward her house. She opened her notebook and practiced her English lessons again.

"Thank you for inviting me to the movies with you," she read aloud.

She glanced behind her. The soldier was struggling to crawl after her, but at least he was moving.

Reshmina kept reading. "It was very nice to meet you. I will friend you on Facebook."

As she walked and read out loud, Reshmina scanned the hillside, afraid that at any moment a Taliban fighter would jump out from behind some bush or twisted tree and kill both her and the soldier behind her. It was silly—she could see no one else was around. But if she was caught . . .

At last Reshmina reached her house. The American soldier was still struggling, but he was with her. She led him into the goat pen out back and latched the gate.

"Stay here until I bring my father," Reshmina whispered. "You are safe."

The soldier didn't answer. He was too exhausted. He lay motionless on the ground as the goats butted him gently.

Reshmina ran inside the house. Her grandmother still sat in the women's room doing needlework, and Zahir played in a corner.

"Anaa! Where's Baba? I need him!" Reshmina cried.

"He just left to go down to the fields," her grandmother said. "What—?" she began to ask, but Reshmina was already running out the front door and down the stairs. Baba was slow on his crutch, and Reshmina quickly overtook him.

"Baba! Baba! Come quickly, please!" she shouted. "There's something I have to show you!"

Baba nodded, looking concerned, and Reshmina hurried him back to the goat pens. Baba stopped short and gasped when he saw the American soldier lying facedown in the dirt.

"How did this man come to be here?" Baba asked.

"I don't know, Baba," Reshmina said. "He must have followed me home when I was collecting wood."

Baba's eyes narrowed. Reshmina knew he saw right through her simple lie.

"I didn't touch him, Baba," Reshmina said. "He was hurt, and he asked me for help, and I came looking for you right away," she explained. "Shouldn't we help him, Baba? Isn't that Pashtunwali?"

Baba sighed. He suddenly looked older to Reshmina than he ever had before, and her heart broke at the thought of bringing more hardship to him. She knew just how dangerous it would be to harbor an American soldier in their home. But Reshmina also knew her father was an honorable man.

"If this man has asked for refuge, he will have it," Baba said at last.

Reshmina clasped her father's hand in gratitude. Then she held Baba's crutch for him as he helped the American soldier to his feet. Together, Baba and the soldier hobbled into the house, Reshmina trailing behind them.

Anaa looked up from her needlework, and her eyes went wide. "Oh dear," she said.

"Mor jani, help me," Baba said to his mother, and Anaa quickly stood and spread a sleeping mat on the floor. The American soldier let out a groan of pain as Baba lowered him onto it.

"Where are we?" the American asked, turning his head. "What's happened?"

"This is my home," Reshmina told him. "You are safe. I am Reshmina, and my father and grandmother are here."

Anaa leaned over and peered at the soldier's wounds.

"Thank you," the soldier said. "My name's Taz." He put his head back wearily on the sleeping mat, then suddenly jerked up again. "Wait—did I lose it?" he asked. He patted at his chest until his hands found the brown stuffed animal attached to his vest.

Reshmina blinked. She'd seen that stuffed creature before. This was the American soldier who'd led the search of their house!

The soldier seemed to relax when he found the toy.

"What is that?" Reshmina asked him.

"My Tasmanian Devil," said Taz. "He's kind of my good luck charm."

Reshmina frowned. The word *Tasmanian* meant nothing to her. She knew the word *devil*, but the thing didn't look like any devil she'd ever seen.

"Is this what Americans think the devil looks like?"

Taz grunted a laugh. "No. He's a cartoon character. He spins around and destroys things."

Reshmina didn't know what a cartoon was, but destroying things certainly sounded American.

"That's why they call me Taz," he added. "For my Tasmanian Devil."

Reshmina noticed that the word LOWERY, not Taz, was sewn on Taz's vest. Most Afghans didn't have family names, but Reshmina knew from her teacher that many other people in the world used them. Lowery must have been this soldier's family name.

"And what does *D-T-V* mean?" Reshmina asked. The letters were tattooed on Taz's arm.

"Oh," Taz said. He pulled his arm against his chest to hide the tattoo, as though he were embarrassed by it. "It means . . . Damn the Valley. It's kind of my company's slogan. This valley—it kills our friends and ruins our lives," he said sadly.

"Yes," Reshmina said quietly. "It is the same for us."

"Will he live, Mor jani?" Baba asked Anaa.

Anaa looked up from Taz's bloodstained leg. "I don't know," she said. "He is badly wounded and needs a hospital."

Reshmina knew that wasn't going to happen. The nearest hospital was in Asadabad, more than a day's walk through mountains full of Taliban.

Marzia came in from the front room with an armful of wet clothes. She saw the American soldier laid out on the mat, dropped the clothes on the dirt floor, and screamed.

"Foolish girl!" Mor scolded, following on Marzia's heels. "Now we'll have to wash those all over again!"

Mor froze when she saw the American soldier. Taz

seemed to sense that he had been discovered by the rest of the family and stayed tensely quiet.

"No!" her mother cried. "No no no no no!"

Reshmina gulped. She'd known her mother would be furious. But Reshmina *had* to help him. It was Pashtunwali. Her mother had to understand.

"He asked me for help," Reshmina said.

Mor's eyes flashed to Reshmina. *"Reshmina, you foolish girl,"* she hissed, *"you have brought death to this family! You have brought death to this entire village!"*

Her mother's words stung as if she had slapped her. Reshmina tried to argue, but her mother turned and marched back into the kitchen.

The front door banged open, startling Reshmina. A moment later, her brother's voice came from the front room.

"Everybody! You'll never guess what happened!"

Pasoon! He was back. A chill ran down Reshmina's spine. She had never feared her brother before. But lately, Pasoon had grown angrier and angrier about the Americans. If he saw Taz in their house now, there was no telling what he would do.

Reshmina ran into the front room to intercept her brother.

"The Taliban ambushed the Americans and the ANA, just like they said they would!" Pasoon crowed. He circled the room, wrapped up in the memory of what he'd seen. "They killed them all and dragged their bodies away!"

Reshmina bit off a gasp. The Taliban wouldn't distinguish between soldiers and their translator—especially not a female one. That meant that Mariam—

Reshmina hiccuped a sob, and then swallowed her grief. She couldn't let Pasoon think she was crying over dead Americans.

"They even shot down an American helicopter with an RPG!" Pasoon said. He mimicked the sound of a rocket-propelled grenade streaking across the sky. "*Shhhhhhhhhhh—*"

Pasoon paused before he could say "Boom." Over Reshmina's shoulder, he caught sight of Anaa, Baba, and Marzia huddled in the next room. "What's going on?" he asked.

Reshmina tried to move to block his view, but Pasoon pushed past her. Reshmina raced after him but it was too late. Her brother stopped and glared down at the American soldier, his face twisting into an angry scowl.

"*What is* that *doing here?*" he cried.

"He's wounded. He can't see," Reshmina said. "He needed help."

"Did you *touch* him?" Pasoon cried.

"No! He followed me here!" Reshmina turned to her father for help. "But it's Pashtunwali to help him, isn't it, Baba? To give him refuge, even if he's an enemy?"

"So is revenge!" said Pasoon. "Or have you forgotten that they killed our sister?"

Reshmina glanced over at Taz. It was clear that the American didn't understand what the family was saying, but he could sense they were arguing.

"*He* didn't kill her," Reshmina said.

"If he didn't do it, his people did!" Pasoon said. "He probably killed somebody *else's* sister. We should turn him over to the Taliban!"

"No!" Reshmina cried.

"Enough," said Baba. "This man has asked us for our help, and so we will help him."

Reshmina raised her chin to her brother, triumphant.

"I can't believe it!" Pasoon cried. "*They're* the terrorists here. All of them. They just call it a war. And you let one of the terrorists into our house! If you're not going to tell the Taliban, I am."

"No, you're not," Baba told him. "While you live under my roof, you live by my rules."

"Then I no longer live under this roof!" Pasoon yelled, and he stormed out the back door.

Reshmina started to follow him, but Anaa reached out for her hand.

"Let him go, Mina-jan," she said. "He just needs to blow off a little steam."

Reshmina nodded. Pasoon had often stormed out

after arguing with Baba, and he always came back.

But what if this time was different?

"Reshmina?" Taz asked at last. "Are you there? What's going on?"

"I am here," Reshmina said in English. "My father offers you refuge in our house."

"I thought I heard someone say Taliban," Taz said. "He's not going to turn me over to them, is he?"

Reshmina translated Taz's question for her father.

"Tell him that even if there are only women and children left alive to fight in our village, we will not let the Taliban take him," Baba said to Reshmina. "He is under our protection now."

Women and children might be all that *were* left, Reshmina thought, along with a few old and wounded men. The very people they were swearing to protect Taz from were the village's sons and nephews and brothers who had left to join the insurgents in the mountains.

Reshmina translated her father's assurances for Taz.

"I—Wow. Tell him thank you. *Manana*," Taz said in badly accented Pashto. "Thank you."

"There is no guarantee the Taliban will respect Pashtunwali," Baba said, "and the longer this man stays here, the longer he is a danger to himself and us. He must be returned to his people as soon as possible."

"My friends will come looking for me," Taz said. "The other soldiers who were with me."

"The other soldiers are dead," Reshmina told him. She hated to be so blunt, but she didn't have the words to say it more gently. "So is an Apache," she said. She didn't know the English word for *helicopter*, but she knew Taz would understand. Her teacher had taught her that the Americans named their flying deathships after other tribes they had conquered.

"The Taliban killed them all and took their bodies," Reshmina said. "I am sorry."

Taz lay back, stunned. "The other American? Him too?"

"I think so, yes," said Reshmina.

Tears welled in the corners of Taz's blackened eyes. "That guy was my brother," Taz said. "They all were. And today, of all days."

"The Afghans? And the woman also? Mariam? She was your brother?" Reshmina asked.

"Not really my brothers. I trained with those men, that woman, for a long time. They were like my family. My people. Do you understand?"

"Your tribe," Reshmina said.

"Yes," said Taz. "My tribe." He wiped his eyes. "Tell your father my radio is broken, and if my people think the Taliban killed me and took me away, they won't come back here looking for me."

Reshmina translated for her father, and Baba nodded. "I must go and tell the other families in the village," he said. "They must know what we have done. Then I will go to the ANA base and tell them this American is here. They can let the Americans in Asadabad know."

Reshmina looked at her father in surprise. The base was almost five kilometers from here. It would be a hard journey on foot for anyone, let alone a man on a crutch.

"Someone else should go, Baba," Marzia told him, speaking up for the first time since she'd seen Taz.

Their father shook his head. "It must be me. Our family has offered this man refuge. He is our responsibility."

Reshmina felt a jumble of emotions. She would have gladly gone in Baba's place, but no family would ever send a daughter to an army base alone. Pasoon could have gone instead, but he had made it clear he no longer stood with his family.

Reshmina turned back to Taz and explained in English what her father planned to do. Taz thanked him again and pulled the strip of cloth that read LOWERY off his uniform with a loud ripping sound. "Give this to your father," he said. "I'm special forces, assigned to advise the base he's going to. Tell him to show this to the Afghan soldiers there, and they'll know I'm really here."

Baba took the strip of cloth from Reshmina. "Keep Zahir in the room whenever one of you is with the soldier," he said, and she understood. Neither she nor

Marzia nor Anaa nor her mother would be allowed in the same room as Taz without a male member of the family as a chaperone. Zahir was hardly a helpful escort, but he still counted.

Baba left the house, and Taz lay back to rest. Anaa sent Marzia for hot water and a cloth to clean Taz's wounds, and Mor called angrily from the kitchen for the firewood Reshmina was supposed to have collected.

"The firewood!" Reshmina said. Twice today her chores had been interrupted. "I'll be back," she told Anaa, then said the same to Taz in English.

He was already asleep.

"Marzia and I will watch over him," Anaa told her, and Reshmina ran out the back door.

The goats bleated at her, angry they hadn't been taken up into the mountains to graze. Reshmina stopped. Where *was* Pasoon? When her brother wanted to go somewhere and be mad, he disappeared into the hills with the goats and didn't come back until he'd calmed down.

What if this time he really *had* gone to join the Taliban?

No. Reshmina couldn't believe he'd do it. Still, something itched at the back of her brain. Today had been different in so many ways—the raid, the woman translator, the American soldier in their home.

What if Pasoon seeing Taz really was the last straw for her brother?

There was one sure way to know.

Reshmina ran around the side of the house, her heart hammering in her chest. Halfway along the wall sat an upside-down white plastic bucket. Reshmina climbed on top of it, reached as high as she could, and found the little hole in the wall where Pasoon always hid his toy airplane.

It was empty.

Reshmina knew Pasoon had put the plane back after the Americans left. Of the few things Pasoon owned, that toy was the one thing her brother would never leave behind.

If it was gone now, Pasoon was too.

Gone to join the Taliban and tell them Taz was alive and hiding in their home. If Pasoon got to the Taliban before their father got to the ANA base . . .

Reshmina hopped off the bucket and sprinted for the goat path that led up into the mountains. She didn't go back to tell anyone where she was headed. She didn't have time.

Reshmina had to catch her brother and stop him from joining the Taliban.

BRANDON

ROCK TO FAKIE

Brandon stopped to catch his breath. The narrow stairwell was well lit, with white walls and gray steps outlined in what looked like glow-in-the-dark paint. Railings ran down both sides, and at each floor there was a metal door and a small sign telling you where you were.

This was Stairwell A, and right now Brandon had it all to himself. It was hot and stuffy, and there was a tinge of smoke in the air. Sweat beaded on Brandon's forehead, and he wiped it away. He was only on the 87th floor.

It was time to get moving again.

Brandon wasn't in bad shape. He loved skateboarding for hours every weekend, and at third-grade field day last year he had won the obstacle course race—forward *and* backward. But walking up steps in this heat was more tiring than any of that.

Brandon's foot splashed on the next step, and he froze. Something clear and wet was running down the stairs from above. It looked like water, but Marni's husband had said a jet plane accidentally hit the building. What if this wasn't water at all, but something more dangerous? Like jet fuel?

Whatever the stuff was, more of it came cascading down the stairs, creating a little waterfall, and suddenly Brandon was surrounded. He couldn't go up or down without splashing through it, and he had to go up, to get to his dad.

Hand squeezing the railing, heart thumping, Brandon bent down low to sniff at the liquid.

Nothing. It didn't smell like anything. Especially not gas. Brandon actually liked the smell of gasoline—it reminded him of go-carts and fishing boats—and this liquid had no hint of gas. It was water, Brandon guessed. Maybe from the sprinklers that had to be going off wherever the fire was.

Was Windows on the World on fire? Was his dad all right?

Brandon felt another terrible pang of guilt at having left without telling his dad. Was his father up there somewhere, searching floor after floor to find him? Was he calling 911 to tell them his son was lost?

They were a team, and Brandon had let the team down. Again.

Brandon's dad had done his best to keep them afloat after his mom died. His dad had often gone the extra mile too, like when he'd bought Brandon a new skateboard even though money was tight, or when he'd stayed up late helping Brandon with his math homework.

Brandon wanted so desperately to tell his dad he was sorry. For running off today, for getting suspended, for everything he'd ever done to make things harder for him.

He would just have to make it back up to Windows on the World and tell him.

Brandon set his teeth and lifted a foot to climb to the next step. He was careful not to splash whatever was running down the stairs onto his jeans, just in case.

At the next turn in the stairs, there were cracks in the wall. At the turn after that, the walls had *fallen down* on the stairs.

Pieces of drywall lay on the stairs in huge, smashed chunks, blocking Brandon's way. Both railings were useless now—one was torn off, the other buried. The metal studs that the drywall had been attached to stood bare and exposed, and red and black wires hung where the fluorescent lights used to be.

Brandon felt panic rising in him. This was bad.

Really bad. Was he getting close to the spot where the airplane had hit? What if he couldn't get past it?

Brandon made himself calm down. He was just going to have to climb over the wreckage. He could do this. He grabbed an exposed end of drywall and hauled himself up. The water flowing down the steps turned everything into a slick sludge and Brandon's sneakers slipped as he climbed, but he was making it.

He was almost to the next flight when the piece of drywall he was clinging to snapped off in his hand. Brandon went flying, slipping and tumbling head over heels back down the stairs. He whacked his head and banged his shin, and with a *thunk* that rattled his teeth he slammed into the wall of the landing, right back where he'd started.

"Crap," Brandon muttered. "Crap crap crap crap crap."

He lay sprawled among the broken drywall. One whole side of him was scraped up, and when he wiped his nose, he came away with blood. There was a nasty-looking purple bruise starting on his shin, and the left side of his stomach was sore when he tested it.

Brandon put his head back and closed his eyes. Except for the smoke and the gritty, nasty drywall, he might have been back in the cement drainage ditch where he'd first learned to skateboard—right down to the trickle of water soaking his butt through his jeans.

All that was missing was his helmet and pads.

But the thing he'd learned about skateboarding was that if you gave up after you took a fall, you were never going to be a skater. You *always* crashed, even when you got good at skateboarding. That was just part of it. Every skater ate pavement. You learned how to fall.

And you learned how to get back up again.

Brandon pulled himself up out of the soggy Sheetrock and started the climb again, more carefully now. He made it to the 88th floor, and through one of the cracks in the wall he saw the red-and-orange glow of a fire.

Brandon felt a mix of fear and relief. *Okay*, he thought. *If this is where the fire is, down here on the 88th floor, then my dad is all right! If I can just get past this floor, I can get to Windows on the World and we can wait for the fire department together!*

With renewed energy, Brandon scrambled up the next mountain of broken and disintegrating drywall. But when he got to the landing of the 89th floor, he couldn't go any farther.

The stairwell above the 89th floor was gone. Not just the walls—*everything*. The stairs themselves seemed to have collapsed in a pile of concrete and twisted metal.

There was nothing to climb, and no going past it.

The entire stairwell was gone.

Brandon's mind reeled. How was this possible? This

was the *World Trade Center*. The biggest building in New York. The second-biggest building in the whole United States. It couldn't just fall apart!

Brandon tried to think. This stairwell was destroyed, but there had to be other stairwells, right? If this was Stairwell A, there had to be a Stairwell *B*, or why would you even label it Stairwell A to begin with? So he could just exit onto the 89th floor, find one of the other intact stairwells, and keep going up.

Brandon took a deep breath and nodded to himself. This was a good plan. This would get him back to his dad.

The door to the 89th floor was a little bent, the way a cheap plastic chair warped when somebody big sat in it, and broken Sheetrock crowded the floor in front of it. Brandon kicked at the wet drywall to clear a path, then pulled on the bent door.

It wouldn't budge.

Brandon put his feet on the wall, going vertical like he was doing a rock to fakie, a skateboarding trick where you came all the way to the top of the half-pipe, popped half your board over the rim, and then rolled down again backward. Brandon pulled with his arms and pushed with his legs, and with a wet screech the door scraped open just far enough for him to squeeze through.

Brandon jumped down to his feet and panted.

Through the narrow opening in the doorway, he could see bright light and feel a blast of fresh air. *Yes. Score one for the skaters.*

Brandon slipped sideways through the gap and froze.

The 89th floor was gone.

Brandon was staring straight out into open sky.

RESHMINA

J IS FOR JIHAD

Reshmina paused at the top of a ridge to look out at the mountains that swept up through Afghanistan and into China. The enormous mountains always humbled her. It was easy to see only the village you lived in and not the wider world if you never stopped to look up.

What Reshmina didn't see anywhere was Pasoon.

It wasn't hard to hide out in these mountains. That was why the Taliban were so difficult to find and fight. Pasoon had to be out there, just over the next hill, just beyond the next valley.

But where exactly was Pasoon *going*? Reshmina started walking again as she considered the question. It wasn't like the Taliban had a village or a camp or a base. They roamed the barren mountains and passes between here and Pakistan, slipping back and forth over the unguarded, unmarked border like they owned the place. Pasoon could be headed in that general direction, like Reshmina was, but how could he be sure he would find them?

Suddenly Reshmina remembered another time when she had followed her brother up into these mountains. What was it—a year ago? Two?

Pasoon had invited Reshmina to go exploring in the mountains, and Reshmina had been thrilled to skip out on her chores and go with him. Pasoon had picked up a stick along the way and was swinging it like a sword. Reshmina strolled beside him, naming things in English. *Rock. Tree. Sun. Brother.* Reshmina couldn't remember a day so fine, a time she was so happy.

They passed a big rock with a Pakistan phone number painted on it—a recruitment sign for anyone who wanted to call and join the Taliban—and she and Pasoon followed the goat path up and around the mountain, higher and higher.

At last they came to a flat space at the top of a steep cliff, and there, leaning against a rock, was an old wooden rifle.

Reshmina gasped. The rifle was scarred and dented from years of fighting, but it still looked usable. Pasoon went right to it, like he'd always known it would be there. It was heavy for him, but Reshmina knew he had used a rifle before to hunt cranes and quail with Baba.

She watched as her brother slid the bolt back to see if the rifle was loaded.

There were two cartridges of bullets on the ground, and Pasoon loaded them into the top of the rifle and slid the bolt back in place.

"Pasoon, what are you doing?" Reshmina asked, suddenly alarmed. "That's not yours."

"No, it's the Taliban's!" Pasoon said. "Darwesh and Amaan said they'd give me five American dollars to shoot at the American camp!"

Reshmina felt the blood drain from her face. Now she understood. Pasoon hadn't stumbled on this rifle by accident, and he hadn't invited her along to "go exploring." He'd known exactly where he was going, and what he was going to do when he got there!

Legs shaking, Reshmina inched forward to look over the side of the mountain.

Across the valley sat a ragtag collection of plywood and plastic tarps clinging to a small, flat space that had once been a logging camp. It was a small American base. Deliberately planted in the heart of Taliban territory to invite them to attack it.

Pasoon took aim with the rifle, meaning to do exactly that.

Reshmina grabbed the stock of the rifle and tried to pull it away from her brother.

"Pasoon! You can't! They have guns there! Big

guns! They'll kill you! They'll kill both of us!"

Pasoon frowned and yanked the rifle away from her. "They won't even know where I am," he told her. "Besides, I'm not going to hit anything. Darwesh and Amaan told me all I have to do is shoot *at* them. Then they'll jump around like angry monkeys, shooting off their expensive bombs at nothing. They'll be at it for hours, and by then we'll be long gone."

"But why?" Reshmina had said. "Why not leave them alone?"

That scowl that would eventually cloud Pasoon's face every day when he was older set in, and his voice turned sour. "We'll leave *them* alone when they leave *us* alone."

Pasoon steadied the rifle against a rock and took aim, and Reshmina backed away. Why had her brother brought her along for this? To watch? To cheer him on? He had to know she wouldn't do that. Because he was scared? Possibly. Or maybe he had brought her along just so a single boy walking alone up into the mountains wouldn't look so suspicious.

PAKOW.

The rifle kicked when Pasoon fired it, knocking him to the ground. Reshmina covered her ears. Pasoon quickly scrambled back to the rock and hid behind it, not daring to peek out to see what his shot had done. In seconds, Reshmina heard the shouts of the Americans, and then the *tok-tok-tok-tok* of their guns as they fired back. She had ducked low, but Pasoon was right—their bullets didn't come anywhere close to them. The Americans had no idea where the shooter was.

Pasoon giggled behind the rock. "I'll just wait until they think I've gone, and then shoot at them again."

"Pasoon, this isn't a game!" Reshmina cried.

But Pasoon wasn't listening to her anymore. He was having too much fun feeling all grown-up and important.

And that's what he's doing now, Reshmina realized, coming back to the present. The Taliban would tell Pasoon what he wanted to hear: that he was old enough to make his own decisions. Old enough to join them and fight the Americans. *That's* where Pasoon would go—back up to that ridge with the phone number and the gun. Back to the heart of Taliban country.

Reshmina hurried down the goat path into the valley. At the bottom of the hill, young boys from her village played on an old abandoned Soviet tank. The khaki-green tank's treads were broken, and it sat tilted, half-buried in the dirt. Faded black scorch marks still showed where the mujahideen—the Afghan guerrilla fighters—had hit the armored vehicle with rockets more than thirty years ago.

The boys lined up along one side of the tank's cannon and pushed it, turning the turret uphill, against gravity. When the turret was as far as they could push it, they hopped on top of the long cannon and rode it as it swung back down. The boys whooped as the heavy turret gathered speed, and then—*clang!*—it hit the bottom of its arc and threw them all into the dirt.

The boys cackled with delight and got up to do it all over again.

"Do you boys know my brother Pasoon?" Reshmina called to them. "Did he come by here recently?"

"Yes!" one of the boys told her. He grunted as he and his friends leaned into the turret. "And he wouldn't help us push the gun!"

Reshmina sighed. So Pasoon *had* come this way. And there was nothing else in this direction except the Taliban.

The boys squealed as their Soviet tank ride clanged and threw them off again, and Reshmina climbed the next hill.

Away from the river, Kunar Province was dusty and brown, the ground rocky and hard. The few plants here were scratchy and dry. Reshmina spied a boy herding his goats up a mountain in the distance and wondered if they had found anything better to eat. She doubted it.

That should be Pasoon up there, Reshmina thought. A young boy loping along, singing a song to his goats as they climbed into the mountains. Not running off to join the Taliban and fight a war that had begun a decade before he was born.

Reshmina stopped to catch her breath, stepping up onto a boulder and loosening her headscarf to let in more air.

She had begun to lose her twin brother in school. Their first textbooks, the ones they had used to learn their letters in Pashto, were old anti-Soviet primers printed by the United States and smuggled in from Pakistan. The books taught the alphabet, but they also taught the children of Afghanistan to fight back against their Soviet captors. Reshmina could still remember some of the lessons.

K *is for* Kabul, *the capital of our dear country*, the primer said. *No one can invade our country. Only Muslim Afghans can rule over this country.*

J *is for* Jihad. *Jihad is the kind of war that Muslims fight in the name of God to free Muslims and Muslim lands from the enemies of Islam. If infidels invade, jihad is the obligation of every Muslim.*

T *is for* Topak. *"Topak"* was the Pashto word for "gun." *My uncle has a gun. He does jihad with the gun.*

Another picture book followed the adventures of two boys named Maqbool and Basheer, who eventually helped the mujahideen clean and carry their weapons before an attack on the Soviet army.

Even their math textbooks encouraged them to fight. *A Kalashnikov bullet travels at 800 meters per second. A mujahid has the forehead of a Russian in his sights 3,200 meters away. How many seconds will it take the bullet to hit the Russian?*

Reshmina knew that the Americans had made those textbooks in order to hurt their enemy at the time, the Soviet Union. What the United States hadn't expected was that they themselves would one day invade Afghanistan. Now the *Americans* were the infidels they had trained the mujahideen to fight.

Reshmina had managed to ignore the calls to war in their textbooks and used the books to learn her letters and numbers instead. But the pictures of tanks and planes and guns had been far more interesting to Pasoon. And it didn't help when boys like Darwesh and Amaan kept coming back to tell him how great things were in the Taliban. Then Hila had been killed in that airstrike two years ago, and Reshmina had brought a wounded American soldier into their home, and now Pasoon was gone. Unless she could catch him.

Reshmina squinted into the bright sun and thought she saw movement on a ridge across the valley. She put a hand up to block the sun. Yes—it was Pasoon! She would recognize that round head and those skinny legs anywhere. Reshmina's heart leaped. She still loved her twin brother, even if she wanted to punch him in the face.

Pasoon was waving his arms like he was trying to get her attention, and she called out to him.

The tiny figure stopped waving and turned. Reshmina saw now that her brother hadn't been waving to her at all, but to someone up on the next ridge. She scanned the top of the hill.

There, among the rocks, she saw the shapes of four men silhouetted against the light. Four men wearing baggy pants and turbans and carrying rifles.

Reshmina was too late. Pasoon had found the Taliban.

BRANDON

A HOLE IN THE WORLD

Brandon stood on the broken edge of the World Trade Center, looking straight out into the bright blue September sky. Strong winds whipped his hair around his face, and burning papers fluttered down from somewhere above him. Exposed electric wires sparked in the sheared-off walls.

Brandon backed up against the stairwell door, his breath hitching in his throat. To his left and right, what was once an interior wall was now the *outside* wall of the North Tower. Below him, the Brooklyn Bridge stretched across the East River, as tiny as a model train set. He was almost *a thousand feet* in the air. But this time, there was no window between him and the open sky.

The wet napkin Brandon had tied around his face

whipped away into the sky. One long stride and he would join it, falling forever and ever and ever.

Brandon's brain couldn't handle what he was seeing, and he sank, shaking, to what was left of the floor. He knew he should move. Get back inside. But he was paralyzed with fear.

The ledge he sat on followed the wall in both directions, but it was only three feet deep. He stared, horrified, at the emptiness around him. There should have been walls here. Cubicles. Desks. Copiers. Fax machines. Water fountains.

People.

But there was no one. Nothing.

In his mind, Brandon kept seeing himself sliding off the edge and falling eighty-nine stories to the ground. He tried not to think about it, but it was *all* he could think about. First his feet would go over, then his legs. He imagined himself clawing and grabbing at the carpet, sobbing, desperate not to go over the side. He couldn't fall. But the pull of gravity was too much. He was too high up to resist. Over the ledge he would go, and then that terrible, awful sinking feeling as he fell backward, arms flailing, legs churning. There was nothing to grab onto, nowhere left to stand. He was disconnected from the earth. From everything he'd ever known. And then the ground would come rushing up toward him, closer, closer, closer until—

Brandon's eyes jerked open. His heart thundered in his chest and every inch of him quivered, like when he woke with a start from a nightmare. He was still sitting on the floor. He hadn't moved. Hadn't fallen.

But he was going to, if he stayed out here much longer. The wind was a living thing up here, pushing and pulling at him like a cat playing with a toy. Brandon had to get up, get out. The whole 89th floor wasn't gone. He could see that now as his senses returned to him. There was still part of it, off to the sides and behind him. If he crawled along the broken hallway, he could make it around the corner, try to find the other stairwell. But his arms and legs were lead. He couldn't make them move.

Whoomp-whoomp-whoomp-whoomp. Air pounded against Brandon and the floor juddered underneath him. Suddenly a blue-and-white helicopter rose up right in front of where he sat. The helicopter hovered, rotating back and forth to hold its position, and Brandon saw the letters *NYPD* written in white on its side. How often had he seen a New York Police Department helicopter flying by overhead and wondered what trouble they were headed for?

Now *he* was the trouble.

Brandon put a hand up to keep the wind from his eyes, and as the helicopter blocked the sun, he saw two people inside it, a man and a woman in dark blue uniforms wearing helmets and sunglasses. Brandon's arms came to life, and he waved them over his head like someone stranded on a desert island trying to catch the attention of a passing ship. The helicopter pilot put a hand to the microphone that bent around from the side of his helmet, like he was talking to someone, telling someone about Brandon. They had definitely seen him! They were going to help! Brandon almost laughed for joy.

But the longer the helicopter hung there, the longer Brandon smiled and waved his hands, the more he realized that there was nothing the police helicopter could do. It wasn't like they could land anywhere here on the 89th floor, or even get close enough to lower him a rope or a ladder. There they were, safe in their helicopter, and here he was, on the edge of a broken, burning building, with a thousand-foot-deep gulf between them.

Brandon lowered his hands and slumped against the door. He might as well have been on the moon for all they could do to help him.

The people in the helicopter must have been thinking the same thing. The woman pulled off her sunglasses, and Brandon could see the anguish in her eyes. She knew Brandon couldn't hear her, not through the window of the helicopter, not over the thundering blades and the roar of the wind, but she said something anyway.

It might have been "I'm sorry."

The helicopter turned and flew away, and Brandon

lifted a hand goodbye. Maybe they could help someone else. Maybe they could help his father get off the roof—and Brandon too, if he could get up there.

Brandon's arms and legs obeyed him once again, and he knew he had a decision to make. He had to move from this spot, get off this ledge. But which direction should he go? The easiest thing to do, the *sanest* thing, was slip back through the door behind him into the safety of the stairwell. But the only way that stairwell went anymore was down, and his father was up. There were two other stairwells though, and if one of them went up from this floor, Brandon might still be able to get to Windows on the World.

He had to try.

Brandon wiped tears from his eyes. The ledge he was on extended all the way along the interior wall to the south side of the building, which was still intact. Black smoke poured from the open hallway, but all Brandon had to do was crawl ten or fifteen feet along the ledge and he would be on solid ground again.

Brandon took a deep breath and maneuvered himself onto his hands and knees, his whole body shaking wildly. He wanted to close his eyes but couldn't—he was afraid to even blink for fear of falling over the edge. He kept his eyes down, ignoring the open sky and the falling papers and the dangling wires. One hand in front of the other, one leg at a time, never less than three parts of him connected to the floor, Brandon inched away from the stairwell door toward the south end of the building. His senses were alive to every little thing, every hint of danger, and he picked up on things he never would have noticed before. The grime along the baseboards of the wall. The hint of slime the carpet left on his fingers. The smell of burning gasoline in the air.

The wind whipped Brandon's hair in his face again, and as he twisted his head to clear his vision, a gust of wind caught him and dragged him toward the ledge, knocking him flat on his stomach. His nightmare came back to him then, the invented memory of sliding over the edge, of falling, of leaving the earth, and his heart leaped into his throat. He cried out, an indistinguishable gurgle of fear and despair, and he scrabbled at the damp carpet, desperate not to fall. And then suddenly he was being lifted, dragged—not *toward* the ledge but away from it. Human hands grabbed him and pulled him into the smoke-filled hallway.

Brandon and his rescuer collapsed to the safety of the floor far away from the ledge, and Brandon tried to catch his breath.

"Holy crap, kid! Where'd you come from?" his rescuer asked, and Brandon looked up into a familiar face.

RESHMINA

THE APACHE

Reshmina's eyes flashed back and forth between Pasoon and the Taliban fighters on the ridge. The Taliban had to have seen her brother waving his arms. But they weren't going to come down the mountain to him. He was going to have to go up to them.

Pasoon put his hands down and started to climb.

"Pasoon, stop!" Reshmina screamed. He was too far away to hear her. Reshmina flew down the hill after him. She was going much faster than he was now, but she still had to cross the ravine at the bottom of the valley and climb the hill on the other side. She was never going to make it.

"*Pasoon, you idiot!*" Reshmina yelled. "*Come back!*"

Pasoon ignored her. Up and up he climbed, getting closer to the Taliban.

Reshmina stumbled into the bottom of the ravine. Her brother was already more than halfway up the next hill. He was going to get to the Taliban before Reshmina could catch him.

"Pasoon!" she cried. "Please! Don't go!"

She looked around desperately, trying to think of anything she could do, anything she could say, to keep her twin brother from joining the Taliban.

Whoomp-whoomp-whoomp-whoomp.

Reshmina felt the vibrations before she heard it—*an Apache.* The American helicopter thundered over the hill and down the ravine like an angry animal, swooping so low it blew dirt and rocks up in great brown swirls. To Reshmina it looked like a giant metal grasshopper: green all over, with a big nose, long tail, and folded-up wings.

Only, underneath these wings were missiles and machine guns.

Was the helicopter out looking for their missing soldiers?

Fssssssshoom!

A rocket streaked from one of the Apache's wings straight toward the ridge where the Taliban had been standing moments before, and—*F-THOOM!*—the hillside exploded. Boulders broke loose from the mountain and tumbled down toward Reshmina. She dove behind a rock and cowered as the landslide rumbled by, pelting her with dirt and bouncing stones.

The Americans weren't looking for their soldiers. They were looking for revenge!

Reshmina heard the Taliban firing back, their Soviet-era rifles clanging like metal poles on a corrugated roof. *Tung-tung-tung-tung.*

When the avalanche settled, Reshmina peeked out from behind her cover. Had her brother been hit by the blast? She couldn't see him anywhere.

Pasoon! That idiot. If he was dead, Reshmina was going to kill him.

Reshmina watched the Apache spin, its guns never leaving their target at the top of the ridge. White-hot streaks, as bright as the sun, shot out from underneath it like fireworks. Tracer bullets. They were so fast Reshmina saw them before she heard them. *Tat-tat-tat-tat-tat.* The helicopter descended, getting closer and closer, and the sound of bullets hitting the hillside got louder and louder. Reshmina put her hands over her ears and winced.

She had to know if Pasoon was all right. If he was hurt, the cowardly worm, she had to help him.

Reshmina stood in a crouch and ran up the hill, hands still covering her ears. The Apache hadn't seen her. It kept pounding the ridge where the Taliban had been—*tat-tat-tat-tat-tat.* Reshmina kept her head down, watching her feet on the broken ground as she ran. In a few breathless heartbeats, she was at the last place she had seen her twin brother. Fresh rocks from the explosion littered the ground.

"Pasoon!" she cried. "Pasoon, where are you?"

A hand reached out from behind a rock and yanked her to the ground.

"Get down, you idiot!" her brother yelled.

"Pasoon!" Reshmina cried. Her brother was alive! Reshmina threw her arms around him, then socked him in the arm.

"Ow!" Pasoon cried.

"I can't believe you really left to join the Taliban! You have water for brains!"

Bullets struck the hillside right above them, and Reshmina and her brother flinched.

"We have to get out of here!" Reshmina cried.

The Apache stopped shooting in their direction and roared off over the top of the hill in pursuit of the Taliban.

Pasoon took Reshmina's hand and pulled her to her feet.

"Come on! Let's go!" he said.

The way back down into the ravine was too wide open—if the helicopter came back, it would see them, and it was clear the Americans were in a shoot-first, ask-questions-later kind of mood. Reshmina and her brother ran sideways along the hillside instead, hand in hand, away from the battle.

"You're not supposed to be here!" Pasoon cried.

"Neither are you!" Reshmina yelled back.

Reshmina's feet slipped and twisted on the uneven ground, and she felt a twinge in her ankle. Her lungs burned and her heart felt like it was going to burst, but she kept moving. They couldn't stop.

Reshmina glanced back over her shoulder to look for the helicopter. There was still no sign of it.

"Reshmina, watch out!" Pasoon cried, and she faced forward again.

Open sky stretched out in front of Reshmina, and her heart dropped into her stomach. A cliff!

Reshmina tried to turn, to dig her feet in and stop, and she fell down hard on her backside and lost Pasoon's hand. She'd been running too fast, and her momentum carried her down toward the edge of the cliff. She twisted onto her belly to claw at the ground, but with a strangled scream she felt her feet and then her legs slip over the side. She was going over the cliff!

"Reshmina!" Pasoon cried. He threw himself face-first on the ground and grabbed her hands, halting her before she slid entirely over the edge.

Only Reshmina's head and shoulders and arms were still on solid ground. The rest of her twisted frantically in the wind.

Reshmina puffed and panted, swallowing a scream.

She kicked and churned her feet, but there was nothing under her. Only air. In her mind's eye, she saw herself losing her grip. Tumbling. Falling. She'd had this nightmare before, tossing and turning under her blanket as she fell through the sky, trying to grab hold of something, anything, as the ground rushed up to her, jerking awake in a sweat right before she hit.

Only this time waking up wouldn't save her.

"Pasoon!" Reshmina cried. "Hold on! Don't let me fall!"

Her twin brother grunted and strained, trying to pull her back up. His eyes were wild with panic. Sweat popped out in beads on his forehead.

Reshmina kept kicking her legs, trying to find something to stand on, to push herself back up.

Then she felt it. Not a rock or a ledge below her, but a vibration. It started in the pit of her stomach and moved up her body. The hair on Reshmina's arms stood on end, and then, like an eagle riding a thermal, something big and powerful rose up behind her.

WHOMP-WHOMP-WHOMP-WHOMP.

The American helicopter.

The Apache hovered in the air right behind her, so close that when Reshmina turned her head, she could see the pilot through the windshield. A huge machine gun, bigger than Reshmina herself, hung from the bottom of the helicopter. Wherever the pilot's gaze went, the machine gun followed, as though one was tied to the other.

The pilot looked left, then right. Then the pilot looked at Reshmina, still hanging over the cliff, and the machine gun aimed directly at her.

BRANDON

THE 93RD FLOOR

"Hey," said Brandon's rescuer. "You're that kid from the escalator this morning!"

Yes! That's where Brandon had seen him before. The bald Black man with the beard who had almost spilled his coffee all over Brandon and his dad. It seemed like forever ago, but it couldn't have been more than an hour.

"Looks like it turned out to be a bad day anyway," the man said, helping Brandon sit up. "Name's Richard."

"Brandon."

Richard pulled Brandon to his feet. "What the heck were you doing out there?" he asked. "You could have died!"

Brandon shivered. "I'm trying to get up to Windows on the World. To my dad. He works up there."

The swirling smoke around them made Brandon

cough. Richard held a damp T-shirt up to his own face with one hand, and reached into his pants pocket and pulled out a wet handkerchief for Brandon.

"Here. I brought this in case I found somebody," he said. "Come on. Let's get out of here."

They held on to each other as they made their way, crouching, down the dark, smoky hall of the 89th floor. It didn't feel weird at all to Brandon to be clinging to a stranger right now. It was reassuring to connect with someone else who was sharing in the struggle to survive. It was the kind of feeling Brandon had with his father, he realized. Like they were in this fight together.

They couldn't see more than a few inches in front of them for the thick black smoke, and Richard felt his way along the wall. It smelled like a gas station up here, and the sharp odor bit at Brandon's nose and throat and made him a little dizzy. He held the wet handkerchief Richard had given him closer to his face.

They came to a steel door that was bent like the door from the stairs had been, still hanging on its hinges but folded down on itself like a crushed can. A sign on the door said JUN HE LAW OFFICES.

Richard tried the door. When it wouldn't budge, he pounded on the door. "Mr. Chen!" he called, his voice raspy from the smoke. "Mr. Chen! Are you in there?"

Richard rattled the door handle again, but it wasn't going anywhere. Through the gap in the door, Brandon could see steel beams and ceiling tiles and drywall piled up behind it.

"I don't think anybody can get through all that," Brandon said. "Not until the fire department comes to help them climb out."

"If he's still alive," Richard said quietly.

Brandon felt a chill run through him. So far, he hadn't seen anyone seriously injured by the accident. He knew people had to have been hurt. Maybe even killed. There were whole offices missing right behind them. But to think that there might be a dead man right behind this door, buried in the rubble . . .

"Worked on the same floor as that guy for seven years," Richard was saying. "Every day I'd see him going in his office I'd say hello, and not once did he ever say a word back to me. Only thing I know about him is that he swings his tie over his shoulder when he stands at the urinals to pee. Now he's probably dead. Crushed when the ceiling fell in on him."

Brandon stared at the bent door, wondering what it would be like to have the roof fall on him. To be crushed under the weight of an entire floor. Had Mr. Chen died right off? Or was he still alive under there somewhere, trapped and choking to death on the smoke from above?

"Come on," Richard said. "There's nothing we can do for him, and we're dying out here."

They kept walking, and Brandon saw the door to Stairwell C. Richard went right past it, but Brandon stopped.

"Wait!" he said. "I have to go upstairs! I have to get to my dad!"

"Listen, kid, I don't think you're getting up to the 107th floor," Richard said. "Something bad happened somewhere upstairs. A bomb or something. You saw— the whole east side of the building is gone."

"It was an airplane! A passenger jet hit the tower," Brandon said. "That's what someone said."

"Jesus," said Richard, looking stunned. "Come on back to the office with me. We called 911, and they told us to sit tight until the firemen get here. I've just been out collecting up any other survivors on the floor."

"No! I have to get to my dad!" Brandon protested. He opened the door to the stairs. It was filled with the same kind of debris Brandon had struggled up in Stairwell A, and the clear liquid coming down was a gushing waterfall. But at least the stairwell was still *there*. The way down was blocked, but Brandon thought there was room to scale the wreckage.

"Whoa!" said Richard. "You can't make it up through all that stuff."

Brandon climbed into the stairwell. "I did it before to get up here!" he called over his shoulder.

"Wait, wait! You can't go alone." Richard hesitated,

clearly trying to decide what to do. "All right, dang it. I'll come with you."

It was easier going with two of them. Richard held onto something and pulled Brandon up, and then Brandon did the same for him, working their way through the wreckage like mountain climbers. They didn't talk during the ascent. They were both huffing too much from the effort and from the thick smoke roiling in the air.

Up they went past the closed door to the 90th floor. And the 91st floor. The rubble was its thickest yet at the landing to the 92nd floor, where they paused to catch their breath. The door to the 92nd floor was bent too, and behind it Brandon could see another mountain of debris. It was so hot that sweat poured from Brandon's hairline, and he dragged a dusty sleeve across his face.

"Ever been to New Orleans?" Richard asked him.

Brandon shook his head no.

Richard mopped his neck with the end of the wet T-shirt. "It's like this in the summer," he said. "Only without the smoke. Like you live on Mercury."

Brandon hoped it wouldn't get any hotter. But every hope he had was dashed when they got to the 93rd floor. There was no way up this set of stairs. The landing was completely filled with drywall and metal and concrete, all packed down like a landslide.

Brandon tried the door to the 93rd floor, but it was

hot to the touch. Through cracks in the walls, he could see swirling orange flames inside. The heat burned Brandon's face like a sunburn, and black smoke poured through every opening. The whole 93rd floor was on fire.

Richard coughed through the wet T-shirt he'd pressed against his mouth. "We can't go any higher, kid. I'm sorry. We have to go back down."

"No!" Brandon cried. "My dad is up there, and this is the only way up!"

Brandon slipped and scrambled up the rubble. He pulled at pieces of drywall until they snapped. He tried to dig his way up. But there was just more drywall and steel behind that. And behind that.

There was no way up to his father and Windows on the World.

Brandon felt empty inside. Like the life had been sucked out of his body.

"No no no no no!" he cried, kicking and beating at the wall of debris.

Richard picked him up from behind, and Brandon thrashed in his arms.

"We can't go up, kid. I'm sorry," Richard told him. "That plane must have hit the floor right above this one. Look. It smushed the whole floor. There's no getting past that in this or any other staircase."

"But I have to!" Brandon said. Tears streamed down his face. "We're a team! Me and my dad. We're a team and I left him and now he's trapped up there and I'm all alone down here!"

"I'm sorry, kid," Richard said. "I really am. But we gotta get out of here before we breathe in too much of this smoke."

Richard carried him down, his feet slipping and scrambling, back to the 92nd floor. When they got to a flat part on the landing, Richard finally let him go, and Brandon slid down against the wall and buried his head in his hands.

"I'm sorry," Brandon said, sniffing. Richard had only been trying to help, and Brandon had thrown a temper tantrum like a two-year-old.

Richard sat down wearily next to Brandon and put a hand on his shoulder.

"It's all right, kid. I understand," he said. "Look, there's a dozen floors between here and your dad. That floor where all the smoke was coming from, that had to be where the plane hit. So your dad, everybody in Windows on the World up on the 107th floor, they're all right."

All right maybe, but trapped, Brandon thought. *Above a fire that's burning* up.

"The firemen will put the fire out, and then they'll hack their way up through that mess and save them. If they don't take them off the roof by helicopter first," Richard told him. "He's gonna be all right, kid."

Brandon hoped so. But what about *him*? He and his

dad needed each other to survive. How was Brandon supposed to handle all this without him?

Richard stood and tried the door to the 92nd floor. "Jammed," he said. "No telling if anybody's alive in there, and no getting through. Let's check the other doors on the way back down though, make sure everybody's okay. Then we'll go back to my office and wait for the firemen. All right?"

Brandon nodded. Richard started to pick his way down through the rubble toward the 91st floor, and Brandon gave one last look up the stairs. The 93rd floor was the cut off. No one below it could go higher, and no one above it could go lower. That was the line that separated Team Chavez.

From now on, Brandon was a team of one.

RESHMINA

KOCHI

Pasoon's grip on Reshmina slipped, and she fell a few centimeters before he caught her again.

The American helicopter kept hovering right behind her—*WHOMP-WHOMP-WHOMP-WHOMP*. Reshmina knew that with just one squeeze of the pilot's trigger finger, bullets would tear through her and her brother. Everything she had cared about, everything she had worked for and struggled for, would all be gone in an instant.

"Come on, Reshmina!" Pasoon cried over the roar of the helicopter. "Climb!"

Pasoon shifted his weight and pulled harder on her hand. Reshmina's fear and panic gave her a desperate strength, and she wriggled her chest up onto the edge of the cliff and swung a leg up and over. Pasoon dragged her the rest of the way over the edge, and they collapsed in each other's arms, weary but safe.

Except for the helicopter.

WHOMP-WHOMP-WHOMP-WHOMP.

Reshmina turned around again. The Apache's blades swirled in the air, blowing Reshmina's headscarf back from her hair and face. Reshmina thought she saw the pilot talking into the mic at his mouth. Was somebody far away deciding her fate, the same way somebody far away, piloting a drone, had decided her sister Hila's fate? Reshmina stared into the eyes of the helicopter pilot. Would those be the last eyes she ever saw?

The Apache hung in the air a moment longer, and then, as suddenly as it had come, it tilted and lifted away to the right, leaving Reshmina and Pasoon where they sat on the edge of the cliff.

Reshmina slumped against her brother. She wanted to flop back on the ground and pass out. But the pops and booms of the Americans and the Taliban still fighting behind them meant that she and Pasoon were still too exposed.

Pasoon knew it too. They helped each other up, and with a quick squeeze of Pasoon's hand, Reshmina thanked him for saving her life. Pasoon nodded, and then they hurried along the cliff, putting as much mountain between themselves and the battle as they could.

They followed a goat path down and around the

mountainside, where they ran into an old abandoned logging camp. It was a small plateau where people had once lived while they cut down Afghanistan's towering cedars and pines and sold them across the border to Pakistan. The Americans had shut most of these logging camps down, convinced the money made there was being used to buy weapons for the Taliban. But the move had backfired, in a way: When the loggers were put out of work, many of them traded their chain saws for rifles and joined the very same insurgents the Americans were trying to stop.

An explosion boomed from the other side of the ridge, and a tall gray mushroom cloud spiraled up over the peak. Reshmina took Pasoon's hand again, and they dove behind a pile of old cedars as bullets peppered the logs.

Reshmina wanted to scream, partly from fear and partly from anger. She had just gone looking for her brother! She hadn't expected to end up in the middle of a battle. Why couldn't everyone just leave them alone?

Reshmina stayed flat on her face for a moment, catching her breath. When she finally looked up, she was staring right into the eyes of a camel.

The sight of it was so silly, so surreal after what they'd just been through, that she wanted to laugh out loud.

Pasoon *did* laugh. "Ha!"

Plegh. The camel spit in Pasoon's face.

"Gross!" Pasoon cried, and he wiped his face on his sleeve.

"Uh, Pasoon?" Reshmina said, putting a hand on his arm.

Pasoon froze. There were even more camels sitting behind the woodpile—and people too. Twenty or thirty of them, an entire tribe of men, women, and children, all cross-legged on the ground, staring at Reshmina and her brother. The men were white-bearded and wore trousers and turbans and long tunics like Reshmina's father did. Most of the women wore tunics and pants like Reshmina, but a few wore dresses with full skirts and wide sleeves, decorated with metallic laces and pendants and amulets. Their children huddled among them, the boys wrapped in blankets, the girls wrapped in shawls, unblinking and unmoving.

These people were Kochi, Reshmina realized suddenly. She had seen them before, but only in the distance. The Kochi were nomads. They had no year-round home, instead traveling back and forth across the border from Afghanistan to Pakistan with the seasons, selling rugs they had made and trading the meat and cheese and wool from their goats and sheep and camels.

"Hi," Reshmina said.

The Kochi stared at her and Pasoon.

Rock and dirt exploded from the mountaintop

above them as the battle between the Taliban and the Americans raged on, but the Kochi and their animals didn't even flinch.

"Let's get out of here," Pasoon whispered. He tried to get up and go, but Reshmina pulled him back down.

"Not with them still shooting!" Reshmina told him.

One by one, the Kochi unrolled prayer rugs. Reshmina couldn't believe it—they were going to pray right here, with an American helicopter flying around shooting bullets every which way.

Reshmina and her brother felt obligated to join them. Ordinarily they would have done *wudu*—washed and cleaned themselves with water in preparation for praying. They made *tayammum* instead, using the dust of the ground to clean themselves. God was forgiving and merciful and would still accept their prayers if He willed it. Better to pray than to not pray, their father always told them.

Reshmina fixed her headscarf and stood and bowed, stood and knelt. God knew Reshmina's heart better than she knew her own, and when she sat to ask for forgiveness, she also said a prayer for Pasoon. *Please help turn my brother's heart from revenge*, Reshmina prayed. *Please show him another path.*

Reshmina spied Pasoon's toy airplane sticking out of his pocket, and she snatched it and tucked it away under her tunic while he had his eyes closed in prayer.

She still hoped God would answer her prayers, but it didn't hurt to have a backup plan.

When they were finished praying, an old Kochi woman stood and came over to Reshmina and Pasoon. "Come," she said, and held out a hand.

Reshmina glanced at her brother. His scowl was back. Reshmina knew her brother wanted to be on his way to the Taliban, not playing nice with nomads. But they could still hear the *tung-tung-tung* of Taliban rifles over the ridge. She and her brother weren't going anywhere. Not yet.

Reshmina accepted the old woman's invitation, and she and Pasoon crouched low as they followed her to a small blanket, where a mother and father sat with their two children. The old woman was their grandmother, Reshmina guessed. Chickens clucked quietly in wooden cages all around them, and a baby camel in a tightly bundled blanket twisted its long neck to sniff them. Three baby goats bleated and butted their heads against Reshmina and Pasoon as they sat down.

Naan, rice, cooked chicken, and pistachios were already laid out on the blanket in bowls, and the old woman offered the food to her guests. Pasoon dug in greedily, and Reshmina gave him a swift elbow to the ribs. They had to accept the act of hospitality—to refuse would be a grave insult—but they shouldn't eat too much either. The Kochi were clearly poor, and the rice alone must be very precious to a tribe with no land of their own.

Reshmina took a small piece of naan and a pinch of rice, and nodded her thanks. Pasoon frowned, but he did the same.

Reshmina looked around at the Kochi as she ate. What would happen if the battle between the Americans and the Taliban spilled over the ridge? What would all these people do? There was nowhere for them go, nowhere else for them to hide.

Reshmina seemed to be the only one worried about it. The two little children giggled as the baby goats butted Pasoon for his food. The grandmother worked at weaving a carpet on a small, portable loom, and the father looped and knotted cloth into some kind of satchel. The mother cradled something under her shawl, and Reshmina was surprised to see a tiny baby, wrapped up so tightly in swaddling clothes that it couldn't move anything but its little mouth. Its eyes fluttered closed as it drifted off to sleep.

What must it be like to live this way? Reshmina wondered. To be born under the sky. To be raised on the move, and sleep around a softly crackling fire. There was a charming simplicity to it. The Kochi owned only what their camels could carry, did only what was necessary to survive. There was no walking three kilometers every day to go to school, no fitting in homework around housework. Reshmina doubted any of them could read, let alone do long division. They certainly didn't know what a computer was, and didn't care.

Pasoon appeared to be just as charmed, laughing with the children as a baby goat tried to climb their father's back. Reshmina wished for a moment that she and her brother were both Kochi. It seemed like the nomads existed in their own world, one completely separate from the conflict between the Taliban and the Americans. She knew it couldn't be that simple—that the Kochi had to have been drawn into the war and affected by it just like everyone else. But she loved the idea of climbing on a camel and leaving all of this behind.

The explosions on the other side of the mountain moved away down the valley, and Pasoon stood. "I have to go," he said, and the spell was broken.

Reshmina bowed their thanks again to the old woman and her family, stood, and hurried to follow her brother. She caught up to him just outside the old logging camp and grabbed him by the arm.

"Oh no you don't," Reshmina said. "You're not going to the Taliban, Pasoon!"

Pasoon pulled free. "Watch me," he said, and he kept moving.

Reshmina seethed. Her brother could be so stupid sometimes. "You grew up in a jam bottle!" she told him, following on his heels.

"You're the daughter of a sheep," Pasoon fired back.

"May you be eaten by termites," Reshmina told him. She could trade insults with her brother all day.

"Go home," Pasoon told her. "You're not even supposed to be out without a male chaperone."

Reshmina caught up again and matched her brother step for step. "Well, I have one now," she told him.

"You're not coming with me," Pasoon told her.

"Watch me," Reshmina said.

Pasoon stopped and turned on Reshmina. "There is nothing you can say or do to stop me from going to the Taliban," he told her.

"Oh yeah?" Reshmina said. She pulled the toy airplane from inside her tunic and waggled it just out of his reach. "Then I suppose you don't mind leaving without *this*."

BRANDON

A WATERFALL OF FLAMES

Brandon and Richard came out of the stairwell cautiously, tentatively, scanning the 91st floor. They had seen fire through the walls just above them, but there was no fire here. Not yet.

There were no people either. They went through every office they could get to through the rubble and debris: a shipping company, two banks, two investment companies, a Manhattan cultural council. There were lots of cubicles, lots of desks, but each of them was empty.

Brandon was searching one of the offices when he saw something fall past the window outside.

Was that—was that a person?

Brandon shook his head to clear it. It couldn't have been a person. Nobody in their right mind would jump from the Twin Towers this high up.

Brandon remembered the wind lifting him off his hands and knees, dragging him toward the open edge of the skyscraper before Richard had caught him and pulled him inside. Had someone else been trying to cross a similar divide and been swept away on the wind? He shuddered just thinking about it.

"Hey, kid, you find anything?"

Richard's voice was soft, but Brandon jumped. They had both been whispering, as though if they talked too loud the whole building would come down around them like an avalanche.

"No. I just thought I saw . . . I thought I saw somebody falling past the window," Brandon said.

Richard recoiled. "God, I hope not. No, can't be. Just your mind playing tricks on you."

Brandon nodded. That had to be it.

Didn't it?

A huge crack ran down the length of the floor in one hallway, almost fifty yards long. The hallway led right into the central part of the floor, the one with the bathrooms and elevators and stairwells. Smoke poured out from the elevator banks, and Brandon and Richard held their wet cloths tight against their noses and mouths. It helped, but Brandon's eyes still stung from the heavy smoke.

On the north side of the building, the ceiling had completely collapsed. The plane must have hit somewhere on this side of the building on the floors up above.

"Come on," Richard said. "Everybody's got themselves up and out of here. We should do the same. Let's check the next floor real fast, then get back to our people on 89."

Brandon followed Richard down to the 90th floor. He was surprised to come out of the stairwell and see two people standing in the hall—a white man in paint-splattered coveralls and a Black woman in a business skirt and blouse. They stood near the elevators like they were waiting for one to arrive.

"Hey," Richard said to them. "We're from one floor down. We were checking to make sure you guys are all right up here."

"We are," the woman said. She gestured to the elevator. "But they're not."

Brandon turned to look. The elevator door was open and five people were inside—three men and two women. They were all dressed in business suits, and all clearly terrified. The elevator was full of swirling black smoke, and they ducked and cried out as sparks popped in the elevator's ceiling.

Panic rose in Brandon as he remembered that awful feeling of being trapped in an elevator. Of it sliding. Dropping.

"You have to get out of there!" Brandon cried. He rushed toward the elevator doors, but the man outside in the hallway held him back.

"They can't," the painter told Brandon. "Look at that stuff falling in front of the door."

An eerie, iridescent blue haze shimmered down like a curtain between the open doors and the elevator car, blocking the way in and out. The passengers in the elevator would have to go right through the haze to get out.

"What is that stuff?" Richard asked.

"Fire," said one of the men in the elevator. "It's like . . . a sheet of blue flame."

Brandon was momentarily mesmerized by it. He'd never seen anything like it in his entire life. A steady stream of bright blue flame, like from a super-hot gas stove. What could cause that?

As they all watched, the blue haze dripped more heavily. Soon it would be a waterfall. A waterfall of pure flames.

"We don't want to run through it," said one of the women inside the elevator. "We're afraid we'll get burned."

The elevator groaned and dropped an inch, and everyone in the car screamed. Goose bumps moved up Brandon's arms to the top of his head, and he got the sickening feeling of falling all over again.

"*You have to get out of there,*" Brandon told them. "I was in an elevator when the plane hit. We just barely got out in time before the cable snapped and the elevator car fell down the shaft!"

One of the men in the elevator groaned, and another cursed.

"We called building security," said the woman in the hallway. "They said to wait for the fire department."

"Somebody's looking for something to block the flames," the painter said. "A cardboard box or something."

"Cardboard is just going to catch on fire!" one of the men in the elevator yelled. He was clearly at his wits' end. They all had to be. Another man was pacing frantically back and forth, the armpits of his shirt ringed with sweat. One woman cried with her eyes closed. The other was muttering something under her breath. Whether it was curses or regrets or prayers, Brandon didn't know.

"What about a fire extinguisher?" Richard asked.

"To extinguish what?" one of the men in the elevator said. "The fire's raining down through the elevator shaft. The source is somewhere upstairs!"

The 93rd floor, Brandon thought. He and Richard had seen it. And no fire extinguisher was going to put out *those* flames. Until the inferno upstairs was extinguished by the fire department, it was going to keep on burning—in both directions.

Something clunked in the elevator shaft up above, and the elevator dropped another two inches. The passengers grabbed onto the rails and cried out. One of the men started sobbing.

The woman who'd been muttering to herself stood taller, as though she'd come to some sort of decision. "I'm getting out," she said. Her voice was shaky and her eyes were wide with panic. "I'm going through the blue stuff, whatever it is." She nodded, talking herself into it. "It's just flames, right? I mean, you can run your hands through a candle flame and be fine. I'll just—I'll just be fast."

Nobody tried to talk her out of it. The other passengers parted for her, and she positioned herself in the middle of the doorway. Richard and Brandon and the two other people in the hall got out of her way.

The woman took a deep breath, covered her face with her hands, and darted through the blue mist.

For a moment—for half a heartbeat—everything was fine. And then the woman burst into flames.

She screamed and beat at her burning hair as she collapsed to the floor. Brandon had never seen anything like it outside a horror movie, and experiencing it now, feeling the raging heat, hearing her awful screams, made him want to retch.

Inside the elevator, the other woman screamed and one of the men threw up.

"Roll! Roll!" the painter said, and unbelievably the woman had the presence of mind to do it. Richard beat the last of the flames with the wet shirt he carried, putting the fire out for good. The woman had burned so hot and so fast she had even set the carpet on fire.

"Don't come through!" the painter told everyone else in the elevator. "That stuff's jet fuel or something!"

The other woman in the hallway went running for water. The burned woman crawled over to the wall and leaned against it.

"I think I'm a little burned," the woman said.

Brandon didn't want to look, but he couldn't take his eyes off the lady. Her hair was gone, and her hands and arms were burned. Badly.

"I can't even feel it," the woman whispered.

The woman in the business skirt ran back with a cup of water, but no one knew what to do. She poured some of the water over the burned woman's bubbling pink arm, and the burned lady screamed.

"We've got to take her down the steps," the painter said. "Get her to a hospital."

Down the steps? thought Brandon. They were ninety floors up!

"Can you move?" the businesswoman asked her.

The burned woman wept. Blisters were forming all over her body, but she nodded.

The painter and the businesswoman lifted her to her feet, and she cried out in pain.

"We'll take her down. You two stay here," the painter told Brandon and Richard. "See if you can find something to block that blue flame and get the rest of those people—"

The painter looked back over his shoulder and froze. Brandon turned.

The elevator car wasn't there anymore.

No, Brandon thought. *No—they couldn't have fallen! They were just here!*

His heart in his throat, Brandon edged as close as he dared to the river of burning jet fuel and looked down. Broken cables dangled where the car had been, and the elevator shaft was a big, empty black hole.

The elevator car had fallen. How far Brandon didn't know. All the way to the basement? Wherever it had gone, the four people in it were surely dead.

RESHMINA

THE CEDARS OF AFGHANISTAN

"Give that back!" Pasoon cried, and he lunged for his plastic airplane.

Reshmina was too fast for him. She held it above her head and twisted away when Pasoon made another grab for it.

"Give it to me!" Pasoon commanded. "You're just a girl! You have to do what I tell you!"

"I'm not a girl, I'm your sister," Reshmina shot back, which somehow made sense.

Pasoon swiped for the plane again, and Reshmina danced out of the way.

"You can't tell the Taliban about Taz," Reshmina told her brother. "We gave him asylum!"

"*Taz?*" Pasoon said.

Reshmina blushed. "That's his name. The American

128

soldier. And you can't give him refuge and take revenge on him at the same time!"

"See if I can't," Pasoon told her. "Badal is as Pashtunwali as nanawatai."

Pasoon grabbed for the airplane, but Reshmina was too quick for him again.

"The Taliban don't respect Pashtunwali," Reshmina said. "They've killed just as many Afghans as the Americans have!"

"When was the last time we had peace?" Pasoon asked. "Under the Taliban, that's when. They ended the civil war."

"The Taliban killed whole families for no reason!" Reshmina told him, feeling a flash of frustration. "They made women wear burqas and locked them away in their houses!"

"They give people jobs," Pasoon argued. "Darwesh and Amaan told me."

"Darwesh and Amaan, Darwesh and Amaan!" Reshmina taunted in a singsong voice. "'Darwesh and Amaan told me to jump off a mountain, so I did it!' Do you ever have a thought that Darwesh and Amaan didn't give you first?"

Pasoon's expression turned stormy. "All right. Here's my own thoughts, Reshmina. Do you think I'm going to be able to afford to get married herding goats that have nothing to eat and growing crops in a never-ending drought? No," he said. "Why should I starve when the Taliban pay twenty times what I can make working for myself?"

"They're killers, Pasoon. If you join them, you'll become one too," Reshmina said flatly.

"Have you forgotten who killed the person who gave me that plane?" Pasoon said, pointing at the toy. He sounded calmer now. More resolute. As though arguing with Reshmina had talked him *into* joining the Taliban, not out of it. "The Americans dropped a bomb on *our sister,*" Reshmina said. "On her wedding day."

Reshmina tried to fight off that awful memory, but it came flooding back to her, overwhelming her.

The day had started as one of the happiest days of Reshmina's life. Her sister Hila had been sixteen and promised in marriage to a boy from a neighboring village. It was tradition to escort the bride-to-be to the house of her new family, where the wedding would take place, and the procession was always a party. Reshmina's whole village had turned out for the parade. Married couples walked arm in arm, and young people sang and danced and fired rifles in the air. Reshmina and Pasoon had been nine years old. They'd chased each other around the adults, laughing and squealing at the top of their lungs. Reshmina had finally caught Pasoon and paused to catch her breath.

That's when Reshmina heard it. An angry buzz, like a hornet's nest. She and Pasoon had looked up at the same time, searching the sky for the source of the sound.

Reshmina saw it now in her mind's eye, as clear and sharp as she had seen it that day. An American drone, high in the sky. It was sleek and gray, with wide wings like an eagle and a tail like a fish. She and Pasoon had watched as it flew closer, closer, coming up behind the wedding procession. Something small and black detached from the drone and streaked out toward the front of the parade. Toward her sister in her beautiful wedding dress, surrounded by all her friends. Reshmina remembered the *whoosh* of the missile, the gray trail of smoke behind it, and then—

Reshmina turned away, feeling the heat of the blast on her face all over again as she stood here in the mountains with Pasoon, two years later.

Now that she was older, she understood what had happened. The happy gunshots of the wedding procession had registered as an attack on an American airplane flying so high up that none of them had even seen it or heard it. But that had been enough for an American soldier in some tent miles away somewhere to fire a missile at them with a drone.

"If the Americans can't be here without killing innocent people, they must leave the valley," Pasoon told her now. "Otherwise, there will be jihad."

Reshmina understood her brother's anger. She felt it too. But a holy war wasn't the answer.

"So you're going to leave our family and join the Taliban," Reshmina said. "Leave me."

Pasoon swallowed. "Yes. And not because Darwesh and Amaan told me to. Because I want to."

Reshmina nodded. She had known this day was coming, but a part of her wanted to pretend that things would never change. That she and Pasoon could be young and happy and carefree forever. But they were both growing up fast. Too fast.

A chill went through her, like the winter wind cutting through her shawl.

Pasoon chose that moment to dive forward, not for the toy plane but for Reshmina. He tackled her to the ground and tried to pin her to take the plane away. Reshmina kicked and grunted, but where she was quick, Pasoon was strong. She tossed the plane away instead.

Pasoon scrambled over her, trying to get at the toy, and Reshmina grabbed his foot. Pasoon fell flat on his face in the dirt, and Reshmina ran and snatched up the plane before he could get to it.

"Ha!" Reshmina crowed, and she held the little plane in the air triumphantly.

Pasoon stood, and Reshmina was shocked to see

tears in his eyes. She'd wanted to make him mad, not sad. She suddenly felt terrible for taking the toy from him.

"Keep it, then," Pasoon said. He kicked a rock in Reshmina's direction, a little of the old anger overriding his sadness, and then he turned and walked away.

Reshmina's heart broke. As twins, she and Pasoon knew exactly how to hurt each other. But they had always known where the line was, and when they'd crossed it.

"Pasoon," Reshmina called, following behind him. "Pasoon, I'm sorry."

Pasoon didn't want to listen, and Reshmina trailed along behind him in silence.

There was a graveyard on the other side of the mountain, and it matched their quiet mood as they walked through it. Hundreds of stone mounds dotted the hillside. The larger ones were for men and women. The smaller mounds belonged to children and babies. Some of the rock piles had colorful blankets on them—mementos left by loved ones for the recently buried. Over others bent tall wooden poles with ragged green flags on top, marking the graves of people who had died fighting the jihad against the Soviet Union when Reshmina's parents were children. In some places, the stones were scattered and low, and it was hard to tell there had been a grave there at all.

"So many dead Afghans," Reshmina said quietly.

"Pasoon, if you join the Taliban, you're just going to end up dead and buried under a pile of rocks somewhere."

"So I should wait around to die in our village, like our sister?" Pasoon said without looking at her. Without stopping. "Like Barlas? Like old Nazanina? Like Uncle Mehtar? Baba's leg was torn up by a land mine just clearing a field for planting. If I'm going to die one way or another, I might as well die fighting."

"For revenge," Reshmina said bitterly.

"For freedom," Pasoon told her. "Everybody invades and tries to tell us how to live our lives. The Greeks, the Mongols, the British, the Soviets, the Americans."

"The Taliban," Reshmina added.

"The Taliban are Afghans."

"Yes, but they only became powerful because they were supported by foreigners," Reshmina said. She had learned about it in school. "People from Pakistan and from Saudi Arabia who wanted to tell us how to live. And invaders always beat us so easily because they have better weapons than we do. Greek shields, Mongol bows, British cannons, Soviet gunships, Taliban rockets."

"American drones," Pasoon added.

"Yes, American drones," Reshmina said, feeling a pang of sorrow for Hila all over again. "But you know why we're always behind? Because while everybody else in the world is making things, we're fighting wars. We never get to move *ahead*, Pasoon. We're stuck in the past."

"Infidels and outsiders may conquer us," Pasoon said, still looking ahead. "But they can never rule us. Conquering Afghanistan and keeping it are two different things."

Reshmina huffed. Pasoon wasn't listening to her.

"Why would anybody *want* to rule Afghanistan?" she asked, frustrated. "There's nothing left to rule."

Reshmina saw a dried-up old cedar cone on the ground and picked it up. Once, their father had told them, giant cedars towered over every kilometer of these mountains. Anaa told stories of streets in the capital, Kabul, lined with cedar trees. Now those trees were all but gone. Each invading army had cut down more and more of them, and the Afghans had cut down still more to pay for weapons to drive the invaders out again. Now Afghanistan was brown and rocky and dead. The only cedars left survived in the most inhospitable mountains, places where even armies feared to go.

Is there some life left in this old cedar cone? Reshmina wondered. *Something dormant inside, ready to sprout if given the room and resources to grow?*

Reshmina broke open the cone. There were still seeds inside. She took one, leaned over, and pushed the seed deep into the ground. That seed would grow to be a cedar tree fifty meters tall and stand for a thousand years—if only everyone would let it.

"Pasoon," Reshmina said, "what if there was another way? What if—"

But when she looked up, Pasoon was gone.

BRANDON

SCARS

Brandon's hands and feet moved like they were on autopilot as he and Richard made their way down the stairs.

All Brandon could think about was what had just happened up on the 90th floor. Those people trapped in the elevator. When he'd turned around, they'd just been . . . gone. And that poor woman, burned all over. Brandon felt sick. *He* was the one who had told her she had to get out before the elevator fell.

Brandon stopped and sat down amid the debris, his eyes hollow and unfocused.

"It's my fault," Brandon said. "That lady—she got burned because of me."

Richard stopped and turned around. He looked as sick and sad as Brandon felt.

"Oh, kid, you can't blame yourself for any of that," he said.

"*I* told them they had to get out of the elevator," Brandon said. "That lady ran through the fire because of me. Because of what I said."

"Brandon, if she'd stayed in that elevator, she'd be dead now," Richard told him. "What you said saved her life."

"*Saved her life?*" Brandon said. "She's going to be burned—scarred—for the rest of her life, and all because of me. I didn't save her life, I ruined it!"

"At least she has a life to ruin," said Richard.

Stay in the elevator and die, or run through flaming jet fuel and be horribly burned for the rest of your life, Brandon thought. What kind of choice was that?

What would he have done, if *he'd* been inside that elevator? He didn't know. Tears sprang to Brandon's eyes, and he cried for the burned woman, for the people in the elevator, and for himself.

Richard sat down beside him.

"It's gonna be all right, kid," Richard told him. "How old are you?"

Brandon didn't want to answer. He didn't want to talk. But he choked out a response. "Nine," he said.

Richard nodded. "Same age as me when my dad died in Vietnam. I wasn't there to see it, not like you were just now with that lady and those people in the elevator.

But it wrecked me. I wish I could tell you there's something you can do to make it better, to make it not hurt. But there isn't. You just . . . you just get over it eventually. Because you have to. It scars over, like a bad cut. It still aches every now and then, when it's cold and gloomy outside and you're left alone with your thoughts. But most of the time . . . most of the time you just forget it's there."

Brandon didn't want to forget. He wanted it to hurt forever. How could it *not* hurt forever? He owed it to that burned lady and those dead people in the elevator.

"Come on," Richard said. "Let's get back down to the 89th floor."

Richard worked in an office called Cosmos Services. He knocked on the door, and a woman opened it and let them inside. She shut the door behind them quickly and bunched a wadded-up jacket along the bottom of the doorframe to block the smoke.

"I was beginning to worry that something happened to you," the woman said to Richard as she led them through the reception area. She was Asian American and had long black hair pulled back in a ponytail. She wore gray slacks and a white blouse.

"A plane hit the building," Richard told her.

"We heard. I got my husband on the phone. I couldn't get your wife, but I left a message, told her you were all right." She nodded at Brandon. "Where'd you find him?"

"He kind of fell into my lap," Richard told her. "Brandon, this is my administrative assistant, Esther."

"Nice to meet you," Esther told him. She led them to the office farthest away from the door, with a window that looked south, toward the other Twin Tower. The air was mercifully clearer here, and Brandon took a deep, grateful breath and looked around. Sports jerseys hung in glass frames on the walls, and a framed photo of Richard with a pretty woman and two little kids sat on the desk. This was Richard's office, Brandon realized.

There were two other people in the office with them. One of them was the oldest man Brandon had ever seen up close. His skin was light brown, about the same color as Brandon's, but wrinkled all over. He had white hair mixed with streaks of darker gray, a big bushy white mustache, and thick bristly sideburns. He wore a maroon sweater-vest over a brown plaid shirt, and on top of his head was a dark brown, pie-shaped cap with a button in the middle of it. He sat perfectly still and calm on a chair in front of Richard's desk, back straight, hands perched delicately on top of a polished wooden cane, as though things like planes crashing into his building happened all the time. His name, said Richard, was Mr. Khoury.

"He's Lebanese," Richard explained. "I've heard him speak Italian, Arabic, French, and Spanish, but I don't think his English is very good. He works at the shipping company next door. And this is Anson. He's a software rep who picked the wrong day to make a sales call in the World Trade Center."

Brandon turned to look at the other person in the office. Anson was a young white man with dark hair slicked back. He wore khaki slacks and a white shirt and a red tie. For some reason, he stood ramrod straight in the corner with his eyes closed.

Brandon didn't understand until he came around the side of the desk. In one hand, Anson held a long white cane, about chest high, and in the other he gripped the harness for his dog, a light brown Labrador retriever.

His *guide dog.*

Anson was blind! Brandon reeled. If any of them should be panicking, it should be Anson. But besides old Mr. Khoury, Anson was the calmest one there.

"Can I pet your dog?" Brandon said, suddenly forgetting all the heavy things that had been weighing on him. What a good dog!

"Usually no—not when she's working," Anson said. "But it's okay right now. Her name's Daphne."

Brandon knelt and rubbed the big dog's head and scratched behind her ears. He'd always wanted a dog, but his dad kept saying no. They were gone from the house too much during the day to take care of one, Dad said. Brandon knew he was right, but he still wanted a dog of his own.

At the desk, Esther turned on a radio. "It was Anson who had the idea to look for a radio, see if we can get any news," Esther said. "We'd just dug one up when you came back."

Esther found a station with two morning radio show hosts talking and laughing.

"So get this," one of the radio DJs said. "Reports are coming in that somebody flew a *plane* into the World Trade Center!"

The other DJ laughed. "I mean, I get it. Planes crash. But how bad a pilot do you have to be to run right into a skyscraper? I mean, what is it they say in golf? 'Trees are ninety percent air.' You know what I'm saying? You've got to *try* to hit one of the towers."

"The guy flying that plane must have been drunk!" the other man said. He laughed. "Hey, stewardess! Cut that guy off—he's got a plane to fly!"

"Turn the channel," Richard said, frowning. Brandon knew exactly how he felt. How could anyone be joking about something like this? If they'd seen what he'd just seen . . .

"Do they give DUIs to pilots?" the DJ kept joking. "Hey, buddy! Pull it over! Yeah, I'm talking to you. Land that plane before I—"

Esther twisted the knob on the radio. She found a news station where a woman was talking about the plane crash, and Brandon paid attention, hoping to learn something new about what happened.

"We're still unclear at this point how this horrible accident could have happened. The New York Fire and Police Departments are both responding, and we're awaiting reports from the ground. In the meantime, we have somebody on the line calling in by phone from one of the floors above the accident. Mr. Collins, are you there? I understand you're trapped in the offices of Cantor Fitzgerald on the 104th floor of the North Tower. Can you tell us what it's like there?"

The 104th floor! Brandon immediately perked up, and he and Richard shared a hopeful look. The fire had been the worst on the 93rd floor. If there was someone alive on the 104th floor, that meant people above the impact had survived. That meant Brandon's dad was alive!

"Well, there's a lot of smoke," the man from the 104th floor said. "The elevators are destroyed, and all the stairs down are blocked. We called 911, and they told us to stay where we are and they'll come get us. We just wanted to let our families know we're okay, and . . ."

The interview went on, but Brandon wasn't listening anymore. He leaped to his feet.

"Richard—he's calling from the 104th floor!"

"I know. That means your dad is okay."

"No," Brandon said. "I mean, yes. But *he's calling from the 104th floor.* That means the phones up there are still working!"

Brandon scrambled for the big black phone on Richard's desk. Why hadn't he thought of it before? He could *call* his dad in Windows on the World!

RESHMINA

SON OF A DONKEY

"Pasoon?" **Reshmina called.**

She didn't understand. One minute, Pasoon had been right in front of her, and the next—*poof*. He was gone. But how? The path they'd been following stretched slowly and steadily up the hill. You could see up to the next ridge, and all the way down into the ravine below. And there were no big rocks or trees for Pasoon to hide behind.

"Pasoon, you son of a donkey!" Reshmina cried. "Where did you go?" She spun, looking all around, but Pasoon had completely disappeared. Reshmina started to panic. If she lost him, if he found the Taliban before she'd been able to talk him out of it—

Reshmina started up the path. If Pasoon had somehow made it up the long hill while she wasn't looking, she would see him from the top of the ridge. She ran halfway there, then stopped. No, there was no way Pasoon could have sprinted all that way in the few seconds she hadn't been looking. It was too far.

He has to be around here somewhere, Reshmina thought.

But where?

Reshmina came back down the path to where she'd planted the seed and opened her senses. She scanned the terrain in minute detail, lingering over every rock, every bush. She listened for the slightest sounds on the wind: a snapping twig, a scuffling footstep, an accidental rockfall.

Nothing.

But then—*tink*—Reshmina caught the smallest metallic sound, almost no louder than her heartbeat. She wouldn't have even heard it if she hadn't been listening so hard.

The sound had come from a steep wall of rock along the path. She moved closer to the wall, listening. Watching. *But there's nothing here!* she thought. She put her hands to the rock face, as though there was some kind of secret door Pasoon had walked through. But no.

Reshmina sighed and looked down at her feet. Wait—were those the faint marks of shoes in the dirt? She crouched down low. It was only when she put her head almost all the way to the ground that she saw it beneath the rocky overhang.

The entrance to a cave.

Pasoon, that sneaky rat! The Afghan mountains were full of hidden caves like this. Some caves were no bigger than the snow leopards who liked to sleep in them, but others went *deep* into the mountains, carved out long ago by ancient waters and smoothed into hiding places by decades of jihad fighters. Pasoon must have known the cave was there and waited until she wasn't looking to scramble inside.

The entrance was just big enough for a grown person to squeeze through, and Reshmina wiggled inside. Beyond the entrance there was room to sit up, and then stand—but it was pitch-black and cold in the cave. She waited for her eyes to adjust, but it was too dark. There was only a sliver of light from the entrance to orient herself.

"Pasoon?" Reshmina whispered. The little toad had to be in here somewhere. He could be standing right next to her, for all she knew. But the cave might also go deep within the mountain.

She was going to have to go farther inside to find out.

Reshmina put her hands out in front of her, feeling her way through the darkness. Almost immediately she ran into something about thigh level, and her heart caught in her throat. Wood scraped softly against rock, and there was a clink of glass. A small table, maybe? With something on it? She felt tentatively in the dark. Yes, a table—and in the middle of it, a lantern! She could tell from its shape. And if there was a lantern, there might be . . .

She patted the tabletop until she found it. A small plastic lighter!

Reshmina struck the flint on the lighter, and suddenly she could see her hands. She squinted in the glare. There was a glass lamp on the table like the one Reshmina's family had at home, and this lamp still had oil in it. Reshmina lit the wick, and a warm glow cast light all around her.

Something was stacked against the smooth walls of the cave just beyond the edge of her light, and Reshmina stepped closer with the lantern to see what it was.

Weapons. The cave was filled with them. Rifles. RPGs. Boxes of bullets. Unburied land mines. The metallic sound Reshmina had heard outside must have been Pasoon tripping over a weapon in the dark.

Reshmina brought the lantern down for a closer look. The weapons were made by many different countries. She recognized some of the languages written on the weapons, and others she guessed at: English, Russian, French, German, Spanish, Korean, Chinese. No Pashto or Arabic though. Afghanistan didn't make the weapons. They just bought them and shot them. It was the big countries that made money selling weapons to the little countries. Who they killed with those weapons wasn't any of the big countries' concern.

What would happen, Reshmina wondered, if the big countries stopped selling weapons to the little countries? How would Afghanistan and Pakistan and Saudi Arabia and Iran and the countries around them fight each other and the rest of the world? With bows and arrows? Swords? Rocks? Fists?

Maybe, Reshmina thought, they wouldn't fight at all. Maybe they would spend their time doing something else instead, like building factories and schools and hospitals.

But that was never going to happen, and Reshmina knew it. She knew too, as a chill ran down her back, that what she was looking at right now was a Taliban weapons cache—a big one.

Reshmina turned, and there was Pasoon, standing right next to her. He'd appeared out of nowhere, like a ghost. Reshmina screamed, and Pasoon lunged for the lantern. Reshmina jumped, and the lantern clattered to the floor.

Krissh! The glass lantern shattered, and—*fwoomp*—the spilled oil ignited.

"No! The explosives!" Reshmina cried.

"Help me put the fire out!" Pasoon yelled.

Together they kicked dirt at it, and Reshmina used

her headscarf to beat out the last of the flames. She was still scared that one of the weapons might go off, and now it was pitch-dark in the cave again.

"Get out—we have to get out!" Pasoon told her.

Pasoon scrambled out first, then helped Reshmina through the hole. When she was back on her feet, she shoved her brother, hard.

"You idiot!" she cried. "You could have killed us both in there!"

"You're the one who dropped the lantern!" he told her.

"Because you popped up like some evil spirit and scared me to death!" Reshmina yelled.

They were both shaking so much they had to sit down on the ground.

When Reshmina could breathe again, she turned to her brother. "How did you even know that place was there?"

Pasoon looked away. "Darwesh and Amaan showed it to me."

Reshmina blew out a laugh. *Darwesh and Amaan.* Of course.

Pasoon got up angrily and stalked off up the path.

"Pasoon, wait," Reshmina called. She got to her feet and followed him again. "I'm sorry. Please, stop this foolishness and come home. Mor and Baba need you. *I* need you."

But Pasoon was done talking. Reshmina glared at her twin brother's back as he walked away. Why couldn't he see there was another path? Another future? Why did he have to follow so doggedly in the footsteps of all the other boys who had left home for the Taliban before him?

High up on a ridge, Reshmina spied a familiar rock with a phone number painted on it—the same one she and Pasoon had passed a couple of years ago. The spot she had guessed he was going to all along.

"The rifle's not going to be there," she told Pasoon. "It can't be."

But it was. They passed the painted rock and came to the small plateau again, and there, right where Pasoon had left it, was the same Soviet rifle he had used to shoot at the American army base.

Pasoon picked up the rifle and checked to see if it was still loaded. Apparently it was.

"Pasoon, what are you doing?" Reshmina asked.

Chik-chik. Pasoon slid the bolt back in place and took aim over the side of the mountain.

"I'm going to call the Taliban," he said.

BRANDON

GET OUT

Brandon dialed the office number for Windows on the World from memory, his heart racing.

The line buzzed with a busy signal.

No, Brandon thought. *No no no no no. Please tell me their phones aren't out.*

Maybe he'd dialed the number wrong. His hands were shaking as he hung up and dialed again. He just needed to know his dad was alive. That he was okay.

The phone was ringing. It was ringing! Someone was answering!

"Hello! Hello, this is Brandon Chavez!" Brandon said, practically shouting into the phone. "Is my dad there? Is he all right?"

There was silence on the line for just a moment, and Brandon held his breath.

"Leo!" the person on the other line called. "Your kid's on the phone!"

Brandon waited breathlessly for what felt like minutes. Hours. And then, at last—

"Brandon?"

"Dad!"

It was such a relief to hear his father's voice. To know, after everything Brandon had been through today, after everything he'd seen, that his dad was still alive. Tears streamed from Brandon's eyes, but he laughed at the same time.

"Oh, Brandon! Thank God you're okay!" his dad was saying. "There was this sudden crash, and the smoke, and I couldn't find you anywhere! I didn't know if you were alive or dead!"

Brandon sobbed. "I'm so sorry, Dad. I was going down to the mall to buy those Wolverine gloves for Cedric. I should never have left you. I was in an elevator when the plane hit, and I was trapped. I got out and I tried to get back up to you. But I can't. There's a fire, and the stairs are blocked."

"I'm just so glad to know you're okay," his dad told him. "I went down looking for you, but we can't get past the 100th floor."

The 100th floor? Brandon frowned. If Brandon and Richard couldn't get up past the 93rd floor, and the people up top couldn't go down any farther than the 100th floor, that meant there wasn't just one floor where the plane had hit. It had taken out *seven whole floors*. Were all those floors on fire like the 93rd was? How would the fire department ever be able to put something like that out?

"But that means all those people from the 100th floor up," Brandon said out loud as he realized it. "That means they're all trapped!" His breath caught, and he started to cry again. "That means *you're* trapped!"

"It's okay, Brandon. We're okay," his dad said. He sounded so calm it calmed Brandon down too. A little.

"There's about seventy of us up here," his dad went on. "There was a big event happening on the 106th floor, but we're all together now. It's really smoky, but we're going to be okay, all right? It was just an accident. This old building is tough. It can take whatever the world throws at it, just like me and you, right? You're all right now. That's all that matters, Brandon. *Madre de Dios.* I thought I would never hear your voice again."

"Me too," Brandon said.

He felt so helpless. He wanted to do *something*.

"Do you need us to call 911?" Brandon asked, glancing at Richard.

"We've called them already," his dad said. "They told us not to move. To wait for the firefighters. What floor are you on? Are they up to you yet?"

"We're on the 89th floor. There's other people here, but no firefighters. Not yet."

"Don't worry, Brandon," his dad said. "We're going to be okay. Both of us. Are you with somebody who can keep you safe?"

"Yes. I'm with a man named Richard. He's nice." Brandon looked up at Richard again, and Richard smiled. "He was on the escalator with us this morning. The one who almost spilled his coffee. Remember? He works on the 89th floor."

"Okay. Good. You stay with him until you're safe."

Brandon's mind went back to the inferno on the 93rd floor. The wreckage. The woman who'd burned. "What if the firemen can't get to you in time?" Brandon asked.

"Then they'll take us off the roof by helicopter," his dad said.

Yes! Brandon had seen the helicopter. And while there was nothing it could do for *him*, it could easily land on the roof and evacuate the people trapped in the floors above.

"It's all right, Brandon. We've been through worse," his dad told him.

Brandon couldn't believe his dad was being so calm about everything, especially when Brandon felt so close to freaking out. He'd been able to put his feelings away through most of it, to push on when things were so horrible he shouldn't have been able to think straight. But now that Brandon was still for a moment and finally talking with his dad, all his fear and worry and confusion came bubbling back up, and he could feel himself starting to panic.

"Brandon—Brandon, are you still with me?" his dad asked.

"Yes! Yes, I'm here. I'm sorry. I—"

"Brandon, it's all right. You still have your key, right? To the apartment? You can get yourself home on the subway. You've done it before. If they evacuate the building, I want you to take the subway home and wait for me there. Got it?"

"I can't do this without you, Dad," Brandon said. He was crying again, and he turned away from Richard and the others, embarrassed. "We're a team. You always—"

Outside, through the window, Brandon suddenly spotted something glinting in the blue sky. It was an airplane. A jumbo jet. Larger than life, and flying too low across the harbor, too close. Terror seized Brandon at the sight of something that *should. not. be. where it was*. Esther saw it too, and she gasped.

The plane was coming right for them in the North Tower—*another plane*—getting bigger, and bigger. Too big. Too close. Brandon took a frightened step back—and then the plane's wing dipped and it turned, disappearing behind the South Tower right in front of them. There was a dull *POOM*, and suddenly a bright orange fireball erupted from the side of the South Tower facing them.

Everyone in the office ducked, and Brandon cried out in shock and terror. The North Tower shuddered again, and Richard cursed. Through the phone, Brandon could hear people screaming in Windows on the World. He put the receiver back to his ear, his hands shaking.

"Dad? Dad! Are you all right?" Brandon cried.

"Yes, something just happened to the South Tower, but we don't know what! I didn't see it!"

"It was a plane," Brandon said with growing horror. He didn't understand what he'd just seen. Planes didn't fly into buildings, but he'd just watched one fly straight into the World Trade Center. "Dad, a plane just hit the South Tower!"

There were more screams through the phone as people began to understand what had happened. Richard stood back up and put a trembling hand over his mouth. "Dear God in heaven," he whispered.

"Brandon—Brandon, are you there?" his father asked.

"Yes," Brandon said. He was still trying to process what he'd seen, but he just couldn't make his brain accept it. For one plane to hit the World Trade Center— that was a terrible accident. But for a second one to hit the South Tower . . .

"Brandon, you have to get out of the building right now," his father told him. The calm in his dad's voice was gone, replaced by a breathless, electric fear. "As fast as you can. Do you understand? Don't wait for the fire department. Get out."

"What?" Brandon said, confused. Nothing made sense. What was happening? *What was going on?*

"Brandon, listen to me. *You have to get out of the building.* Now."

"I don't understand," Brandon said. He held the phone with both hands. "Dad, I don't—"

"Brandon, *hang up and get out of the building as fast as you can,*" his father told him. "This wasn't an accident. We're under attack!"

RESHMINA

GONE

Reshmina ran to look over the edge of the mountain where Pasoon had aimed his rifle, and she pulled back in surprise. The American camp, the one Pasoon had shot at years ago, was abandoned now. The Taliban had torn down the tin roofs and painted insults on the rock barriers, but nobody was there. The Americans had packed up and left. The ANA still had bases in the province, but not the Americans. Not anymore.

"Ha!" Reshmina said. "Look! All that shooting, all that fighting, and for what? Neither side won anything, and neither side lost anything—except lives."

"*We* won," Pasoon told her. "We drove them out."

"Out of what? Why? Nobody lives here!" Reshmina cried. "We're in the middle of nowhere! There's no water, no food, nothing for animals to graze on. Nobody really wants this place—not the Americans, and not the Taliban either. They just wanted to fight. It's like it's all some big game."

Pasoon aimed the rifle at the old camp and pulled the trigger.

PAKOW!

Reshmina put her hands over her ears. "Pasoon, what are you—?"

Pasoon fired again. *PAKOW!*

What was he doing? There was nobody down there!

PAKOW! The old Soviet rifle echoed down through the valley.

Suddenly Reshmina understood. *I'm going to call the Taliban*, Pasoon had said. Which was silly, because neither of them had a phone. But if Pasoon couldn't call the Taliban on the phone, he could call them with a rifle.

He'd make them come to see who was shooting.

Reshmina grabbed the rifle and tried to pull it from Pasoon's hands.

"Pasoon, don't!" Reshmina pleaded. "You don't know what you're doing!"

"I do too," Pasoon said as they tussled. "I'm doing what you and Baba should have done in the first place! I'm going to tell the Taliban there's an American soldier in our house!"

Pasoon was too strong for her. He wasn't going to give up the gun. Reshmina tucked a foot around his leg and tripped him, and they fell to the ground with a thud. The rifle slipped from Pasoon's fingers and they fought for it, kicking and shoving and wrestling each other. And not in the playful way they had that morning. This was desperate. Vicious. Reshmina felt like she was fighting for her life.

Pasoon pushed her away with his foot and got enough separation from her to stand. He held the gun to one side, barrel pointed at the ground, and panted to catch his breath. His eyes were wide and wild, and his chest heaved.

"You're so stupid, Pasoon!" Reshmina told him. She pulled herself to her feet. "You're like a worm who crawls into a snake's nest and says, 'Hey, what are we snakes going to do today?' You're just a little baby playing at being a grown-up!"

Pasoon hit her hard on the side of her face with his open palm. The blow was so sudden, so brutal, it sent Reshmina to her hand and knees. Rocks cut into her palms, but she didn't move. Reshmina tasted blood where she'd bitten her own tongue, and her face burned from the sting of Pasoon's hand. But what made her cry was the awful, shocking savagery of it. Reshmina and her twin brother had played rough since they were babies, pushing and poking and yanking at each other whenever they squabbled. But Pasoon had never hit her. Not like this. Not with such venom.

The worm was a snake after all.

Reshmina dragged her sleeve across her eyes, but stayed on her hands and knees.

"Pasoon—" she began, but her brother cut her off.

"I may be your twin brother, Reshmina, but this is still Afghanistan. I am still a man, and you are still a woman, and you can't speak to me like that."

Reshmina kept her eyes on the ground. "Pasoon, you know what the Taliban does to anyone who helps the Americans. If you tell them we're hiding an American soldier in our house, they will kill us all when they come for him. Everyone you love will die. Anaa. Mor. Baba. Marzia and Zahir. Me."

Pasoon's voice wavered as he answered. "Baba made his decision. He's the one who sided with the infidels."

"They will kill everyone in the village just to teach us a lesson, Pasoon. You've seen them do it. The Taliban will kill us all. *You'll* kill us all."

Reshmina heard Pasoon sniff like he was crying, but she still didn't look up. Wouldn't.

"So be it," Pasoon told her. "Whatever happens to our family, it's Baba's fault. And yours," he added.

Pasoon slid the bolt back and forth on the rifle and fired again—*PAKOW!*—into the air. Reshmina shrank from the noise.

He did it again. *PAKOW!*

Reshmina kept her head down and closed her eyes,

waiting for another shot. When nothing came, she looked up again.

Three Taliban fighters were coming along the path toward them.

"Pasoon—" Reshmina pleaded. "Pasoon, I still have your toy," she said, digging it out of her tunic to show to him.

"Keep it," Pasoon told her. "Toys are for babies. I'm a man now."

Reshmina got to her feet. She saw now there was no stopping Pasoon from telling the Taliban about Taz. And as soon as he did, the Taliban would come to their village. They would kill Taz, and they would kill the rest of them for giving him refuge.

The only thing she could do was get back to her village first. She had to warn her family and everyone else.

Reshmina turned and ran down the steep hillside, tumbling and falling and hitting every rock and bush along the way. She slid to a stop in a narrow ravine, but could still see the Taliban up above. They were almost to her brother. Reshmina wrapped her scarf around her head and stumbled away, sobbing. All she wanted to do was sit down and cry, but she had to hurry.

She hurt all over from her rough descent, and her face still burned where Pasoon had struck her. But it was the loss of her brother that hurt worse than anything. Everything they had ever had, everything they had shared as twins, as close as two people could perhaps ever be in this world, was gone forever.

Reshmina glanced over her shoulder one last time. Pasoon was talking animatedly with the Taliban and pointing back in the direction of their village.

Reshmina ran faster.

BRANDON

THE SKY LOBBY

A plane had hit the South Tower. *A second plane.* Brandon still couldn't believe it. But he'd seen it. Flying in, turning at the last second so that it hit the South Tower full on. Not an accident. Deliberate.

An attack.

But by whom? And why?

Brandon was so distracted he almost tripped as he followed Richard and his floor mates down the stairs. They formed two rows, going down side by side: Esther leading Mr. Koury by the elbow in front, Anson and his guide dog behind them following the railing, Brandon and Richard together in the rear. Brandon wanted to *run* down the stairs, to get out of the North Tower as quick as he could, but Anson and Mr. Khoury couldn't go any faster.

"At least the stairs are better than the last time," Esther said. "After the bombing."

Brandon looked up. "What bombing?" he asked.

"Terrorists set off a bomb in the parking garage under the building," Richard explained. "Back in '93."

Brandon's dad had been working in Windows on the World then, but it was no wonder Brandon didn't remember it—he'd only been a year old.

"Was anybody hurt?" Brandon asked.

"A few people died, and a thousand more were hurt," Richard told him. "It was a scary time."

It couldn't have been as scary as today, Brandon thought.

"It took us *three hours* to get downstairs that day," Esther said. "The bomb took out the building's power, and you couldn't see a blessed thing in the stairs. They were total caves. It was chaos. All the smoke from the bomb came *up* the stairs. You couldn't breathe. Now at least there's fluorescent paint on the walls. But they didn't make the stairs any wider."

"Why did terrorists bomb the World Trade Center back then?" Brandon asked. "Is this another terrorist attack?"

"I don't know, kid. Maybe so," said Richard. "I don't know who else would do it. The ones who bombed the building back in '93 said they did it because we kept sticking our noses in the Middle East, and they wanted us out."

"But why the World Trade Center?" Brandon asked.

"It's a pretty easy target," said Esther. "And a pretty noticeable one too. Sticking up taller than everything else around it."

Brandon still didn't understand. What purpose did attacking the Twin Towers serve? Hurting all these innocent people?

Down and down they went. Broken light fixtures hung from the ceiling, and water still streamed down around their feet. But not as much as before. There were more cracks in the walls too, ten floors down from where the first plane had hit. Through some of them, Brandon could see flames. Why were some floors on fire, and others weren't?

They didn't stop to find out.

"You doing okay, Anson?" Richard asked.

"Yes, I'm fine," he called back, even though his voice sounded strained.

"How about you, Mr. Khoury?" Richard asked.

"I too am all right," Mr. Khoury said in heavily accented English.

"You seem very calm, Mr. Khoury," Esther told him. Brandon had been thinking that too. How could the old man be so chill with everything that was going on?

Mr. Khoury shrugged. "In 1978, I come to United States from Lebanon, where these war like this happen when I am young man," he said, waving his hand at the destruction. "I am refugee once. Now I am refugee again."

Brandon didn't understand. The United States wasn't at war with anybody, were they? No—not that he knew of.

But maybe now they were.

Brandon thought going downstairs would be easy. It was certainly easier than going *up*. But his legs burned and his feet ached. All he wanted to do was sit down and rest, but he knew he couldn't stop. Not for long. Besides, if Mr. Khoury could do it, Brandon could do it. Despite his age, Mr. Khoury moved right along at his slow, deliberate pace and never stopped, never complained.

At the 78th floor, they came to the highest of the two Sky Lobbies, where people got on and off the local elevators that serviced the floors above and below them.

This was where I was headed in that first elevator when I left Windows on the World! Brandon realized with a start. How long had it taken him to go thirty floors?

"Let's get out here and see if we can find somebody in charge," Richard suggested, and the group exited the stairwell.

The last time Brandon had been through the Sky Lobby, on another trip to work with his dad, it had been quiet and mostly empty. Now it was dark, smoky, and crowded. People called out numbers—"*86! 84! 79!*

81!"—and Brandon finally figured out they were saying their floor numbers, trying to connect with friends and coworkers. Trying to find out who had made it and who hadn't.

Nobody called out any numbers higher than 89.

"This is a madhouse," said Richard.

The refugees from the 89th floor stayed close, holding each other's hands.

"Should we just keep going down?" Esther asked.

If Richard had been hoping to find a person in charge, Brandon didn't see one. There were no firefighters, no police officers, not even building security guards.

A dull blue light suddenly glowed above the heads of the crowd. It was a man holding up a cell phone. He was using the soft glow to lead a group of people to a stairwell on the other side.

"That guy looks like he knows what he's doing," Esther said. "Maybe we should follow him."

Brandon didn't know how *anybody* knew what they were doing. Not in this chaos.

"I'm with Esther," Anson said. He stood perfectly still, one hand clutching the handle on the harness of his dog, and the other holding his cane. People bumped and cried out in panic all around him, but like Mr. Khoury, Anson stayed calm.

"It was pretty clear coming down Stairwell B,"

Richard said. "I don't know why we should switch out all of a sudden."

"I'm with Richard," Brandon said. He had promised his father he'd stay with him, and besides, he liked Richard.

"We go," Mr. Khoury said, still calm and assured. He, Esther, and Anson moved forward, toward the stairwell that the man with the glowing cell phone had used, not back to the stairwell they had walked down.

Richard and Brandon hesitated. Before they could decide where to go, someone called out, "Coming through!"

The crowd parted for two men pushing another man in a wheelchair. Brandon's jaw dropped. He'd thought it must be hard for Anson trying to get out of the towers. But how terrifying must it be for someone trying to escape in a wheelchair? They couldn't use the elevators anymore, and they couldn't get down the stairs on their own. Just the thought of being trapped like that made Brandon shudder.

The two men had to lift the wheelchair to get it into the stairwell, and a crowd piled up behind them to wait. Richard and Brandon quickly became separated from Esther, Anson, and Mr. Khoury in the confusion.

"Where are they? Do you see them?" Brandon asked Richard. Even jumping up and down, he couldn't see over the wall of people.

"I don't know," Richard said. "I've lost them. I think they went down the stairs before the man in the wheelchair."

Richard took a look at the crowd waiting to go down the stairs and pulled Brandon back the way they had come.

"What are you doing? What about the others?" Brandon asked.

"Even at Mr. Khoury's pace, we'll never catch up to them," Richard said. "Not with that wheelchair between us. Esther's still with them. They'll be all right as long as they keep moving. But we gotta get out of here too, and that line isn't going anywhere. I figure we're better off in the stairwell where we started. You okay with that?"

"Yeah," said Brandon. He hated to leave the others, but it made sense.

"It's just you and me now, kid," Richard told him.

Brandon nodded in the darkness. He was okay with that too.

The people on Stairwell B moved steadily, two by two, down flight after flight. Some of the doors to the other floors were locked, or blocked by something, and Brandon hoped the people on those floors had found a different way out. Sometimes he and Richard would leave the stairs and cross a floor to see if another stairwell was faster, and along the way Brandon would pick up phones on random desks, just in case. Most of them didn't work. The few that did gave them busy signals when they tried dialing Richard's family and Windows on the World. *All eight million people in the city must be trying to use the phone lines right now*, Brandon thought.

With each busy signal, Brandon's panic mounted. Was his father all right? Would the firefighters get to him in time? The first plane had hit the North Tower almost an hour ago, and he hadn't seen a single firefighter yet. And now they had a *second* building to worry about.

Brandon's legs were aching by the time they reached the 44th-floor Sky Lobby. He and Richard left the stairwell again to see if they could find Esther and the others, but things were even more chaotic here.

The 44th floor had become a kind of hospital. There were EMTs and paramedics here—at last!—helping scores of people with broken limbs, cuts and bruises, and burns. Brandon wondered if the poor burned woman from the 90th floor was here, getting treatment, or if she had already been taken downstairs.

People were moving every which way. Some of them were looking for a paramedic. Others were looking for a stairwell. There was a line for the telephone at the security station, which apparently still worked, and the few people with cell phones were loaning them to other people to try to reach their families. Here too, people were calling out floor numbers and names. Brandon looked around for Esther and Anson and Mr. Khoury, but he didn't see them.

Ka-TISSSSH! Something massive crashed into the floor across the room, and everyone screamed. Smoke and debris shot through the crowd. People tried to run, but there was nowhere to go.

Brandon ducked and squeezed his eyes shut, bracing for the flaming jet fuel that would burn him alive. *No!* he thought in terror. *Not another plane!*

RESHMINA

POPPIES

Reshmina crouched low, staring down at a sea of poppy flowers wedged between two steep canyon walls. They were bright and pink, and swayed gently in the mountain breeze.

And they were right in Reshmina's path.

Reshmina carefully climbed down the ridge and stood at the edge of the poppy field. How strange to see such brilliant color here, among all the brown of the mountains. The flowers were so thin, so delicate, and they moved back and forth as though they were people mingling at a party. Like they were dancing.

Reshmina wished she could just sit and watch them. She was tired—pushed to the edge of exhaustion. She'd been running since she left her brother behind, taking shortcuts up and down rocky, desolate hills. She was desperate to get back to her village. If her father hadn't returned from the ANA camp yet, she had to hide Taz so the Taliban wouldn't find him. If Baba *had* returned, and Taz was already gone, Reshmina still had to alert the villagers that the Taliban were coming.

No matter what, the Taliban weren't going to be happy the villagers had given Taz refuge. And it was all Reshmina's fault, just like Pasoon said.

Reshmina walked out among the poppies. The flowers were so tall they came up to her nose. The effect of standing among them, of almost being swallowed up by them, was magical. She wished the whole of Afghanistan were covered with the beautiful flowers.

But Reshmina knew it couldn't be. People didn't grow poppies for their pretty pink colors. Poppy seeds had a gummy substance that was the raw material for heroin. Heroin was a drug that took away people's pain. For many Afghans hurt by decades of war, it was the only kind of medicine they could find to erase that suffering—and their awful memories. Afghan parents had long given the drug to their babies to ease earaches, or in place of food to soothe their hunger pains.

But Reshmina knew that heroin wasn't medicine. It was an addictive, destructive drug that eventually killed everyone who couldn't stop using it. And addicts would do anything for their next fix—lie, steal, even sell their own children.

Poppies loved the rocky, dry soil of the mountains, and it was easy to hide fields like this one high up in the mountains. You could get rich growing poppies for heroin, but you could get in trouble too. The Taliban made a lot of money that way to pay for more guns and bombs, so the United States destroyed any poppy fields they could find and arrested the farmers who had planted them.

Reshmina put her hands out, brushing the stalks of the poppies as she walked, pretending for just a moment that they were nothing but beautiful flowers, not the source of so much agony and heartbreak.

Reshmina's father refused to grow poppies, even though their family was very poor. And with Afghanistan getting hotter and drier, it was harder for Baba to grow real crops, like wheat and melons. Pasoon had fought with Baba about it, of course. Pasoon had argued that they only had to grow poppies for one, perhaps two seasons, and they would make more money than they would see in a lifetime of growing food. It would be easier too—every year there was less water, less usable land, and more chance the food crops would fail and they would earn nothing. Reshmina knew Pasoon was right about that part, at least. But Baba had said growing heroin was a bad business, and against Islam, and that had been that.

Reshmina put a hand to the side of her face, where

her brother had hit her. Tears came to her eyes again, and her heart ached at his betrayal. But it was too late for that now. Pasoon had made his choice, and so had she.

Reshmina remembered her prayer in the Kochi camp, for God to show Pasoon a different path. Her request was a *du'a*. A special request in a time of need. According to their imam, the prayer leader in their mosque, God promised to answer a du'a in one of three ways. The first and best answer was when God gave you what you asked for, right when you asked for it. The second was to give you what you prayed for, but at some later date. The third was to not give you what you asked for at all, but instead to prevent some other hardship or injury from happening to you.

God certainly hadn't answered Reshmina's request by changing Pasoon's path. Did that mean that at some later time, God would forgive Pasoon and change her brother's heart? Reshmina hoped so. But she wasn't sure *she* could ever forgive her brother.

Something red flashed against all that pink, and Reshmina froze.

Patrolling the far edge of the poppy field was a man wearing a green tunic, a white turban, and a red scarf. It was the red scarf that had caught Reshmina's attention, but now all she could see was what the man carried over his shoulder: an old Soviet-era AK-47 rifle.

Reshmina ducked low in the poppies and held her

breath. Had the soldier seen her? She waited for long seconds. Minutes. But no one came.

Reshmina looked around, trying to figure out how she could escape. All she saw were poppies everywhere she looked. She could go back the way she had come, but that would take too long. But if this soldier caught her, there was no telling what he would do. She had discovered his hidden, illegal poppy field.

Sweat ran down Reshmina's back, and her heart thumped hard in her chest. She could *not* get caught. Slowly, carefully, as quietly as she could, Reshmina chanced another peek over the tops of the poppies.

The red-scarf soldier leaned against a rock. He was turned away from her, smoking a cigarette. He wasn't paying particular attention to the poppy field. Or anything, really. That's why he hadn't noticed Reshmina as she came down through the pass. He was just a guard, and it must have been terribly boring to have to sit and watch a poppy field all day long, high up in the mountains where no one else could see you or talk to you. If she waited long enough, he would probably go to sleep.

But Reshmina couldn't wait for that. She had to get past him. Now.

Reshmina inched forward in a crouch, trying to squeeze between the tall poppies without making them move. She didn't know what she was going to do when she got to the end of the field. Throw a rock to distract the guard? Maybe he would wander off to relieve himself, and she could slip by. But every minute she waited was another minute the Taliban might be getting closer to her village.

Snap!

Reshmina pulled her foot back from the brittle poppy stem she'd stepped on and froze.

"Is somebody there?" the guard called.

Reshmina closed her eyes and silently cursed herself.

Clack-clack.

Reshmina's eyes flew open. She knew that sound. It was the guard cocking his rifle. Making it ready to shoot.

"I see you!" the guard cried. "Come out with your hands up!"

BRANDON

LAST CALL

The blast of fire Brandon braced for never came. He looked up and saw Richard crouching next to him. He'd been ready for a shock wave too.

But if it wasn't another plane, what was it? What happened?

Richard stood to look. He put a hand over his mouth and pulled Brandon away as new screams—screams of horror—filled the air.

"It wasn't a plane—it was an elevator," Richard told him. "An elevator just crashed down, and the people in it—"

He couldn't finish. He didn't have to. Brandon could guess without seeing it himself.

This is my reality now, Brandon realized. *I hear a crash, and my first thought is "A plane is hitting the building!*" He never would have assumed that a day ago, an hour ago, but things were different now. He'd gone from a world where planes didn't fly into buildings to one where things like that *did* happen. Now he expected it.

Brandon and Richard hurried back into the stairwell and kept going down.

Everyone seemed to have gotten the message to get out as quickly as they could, and the stairwells were a bottleneck of desperate, frightened people. Their descent slowed to a crawl. Sometimes Richard and Brandon stood on *one step* for a full minute before they got to move down to the next step. All around them, men and women who had cell phones kept trying to make calls. No one could get a signal.

"Hey, so tell me something about yourself," Richard said to Brandon while they waited. "What do you like to do?"

Brandon shrugged. "I don't know. Skateboard, I guess."

"We've got a skate park near us in Queens," Richard told him. "Drive by there sometimes. I see kids doing the craziest things on those skateboards."

Brandon knew Richard was just trying to distract him, but he couldn't think about skateboarding right now. He couldn't think about anything but getting out of here.

Fifteen minutes later, Brandon and Richard were

only to the 36th floor. Brandon could feel his frustration mounting. He and Richard shared a look of despair. But they didn't say anything, and neither did anyone else. No one yelled, and no one got mad. No one told anybody to *get a move on, for God's sake*. For a bunch of New Yorkers who honked if you took a second too long to cross the street, everybody was remarkably calm. Brandon didn't know how they were doing it. He felt like he was two seconds away from screaming.

They hit the landing for the 29th floor, and Brandon sagged with relief. They were in the twenties! Not far now! A man in a delivery uniform stood in the doorway, handing out bottles of water to people as they went by, and Brandon drank his greedily, his throat raw and dry.

Another man carried a glass coffee pot filled with water, with paper towels floating inside. "I've got wet paper towels to breathe through, if anybody needs one!" he called out.

Brandon and Richard kept going. Brandon's legs ached even worse than before. All he wanted to do was sit down.

One man they came to *had* sat down, right there on the stairs. He was older and overweight, and he had clearly been pretty high up when he started his walk down. The back and armpits of his shirt were covered in sweat, and his face was pale and his breathing labored.

A woman stood in front of him, waving a newspaper at him to cool him down.

"Lionel, can you walk?" she asked him. "We have to keep moving."

Lionel stayed where he was.

Somehow the fumes were worse down here, even though they were farther away from the fire above. Brandon's head was groggy, his eyes unfocused. He ran his tongue along the roof of his mouth and realized he could *taste* the jet fuel fumes.

At the 20th floor, Richard grabbed Brandon and pulled him through the door.

"Come on," he whispered. "Let's see if one of the other stairwells is faster."

The 20th floor was empty of people. Computer monitors still glowed. On one, a cursor blinked in the middle of an unfinished sentence. Across the room, a phone rang plaintively, no one there to answer it.

But that meant the phones here were still working!

Brandon's heart fluttered with cautious hope. He was desperate to talk to his father again, but he had been disappointed so many times before when he couldn't get through. He rushed to a phone near a window and dialed the number for Windows on the World.

Richard knew what Brandon was doing and sat down at another desk to try to call his own family.

Brandon waited breathlessly, and then—the line was

ringing! He'd gotten through! Brandon clung to the receiver, waiting for someone to pick up, when something went plummeting past the window.

Not something. Some*one*.

Richard stood from his chair. *"Jesus Christ,"* he whispered.

He had seen it too, then. Brandon wasn't imagining things. A man in dark pants and a white shirt and a light blue tie had just fallen past their window, twenty stories in the air.

"Hello? Brandon? Is that you?" his father said, finally answering the phone.

"Dad! Oh my God, Dad, I just saw a man falling past the window!"

"Brandon, I—I can't talk long," his father said slowly. His voice was quiet. Weak. "Everybody else—everybody is down on 106. We broke a window to get some air. The smoke is getting thicker. But I waited—"

"Dad, you have to get up to the roof! Get to the helicopters!" Brandon told him.

"Can't. Too much smoke," his dad said sadly. "Helicopters can't land."

What? How could that be? The helicopters had to be able to land on the roof! How else were they supposed to get all those trapped people out?

"The floor is groaning. Buckling. Fire's coming up through the floor," Brandon's father said. "No sprinklers.

We already threw the fire extinguisher out the window to break it open for air. Not that it would help."

Brandon realized he was crying. He knew what his father was telling him. He could hear it in the strain in his voice, in the things he was saying. His dad just didn't want to say it, and Brandon didn't want to hear it.

"*Dad,*" Brandon said. "Dad, you have to get out of there." He felt so helpless. He knew there was nothing he could do, nothing his father could do, or his dad would have done it already. But still he tried to think of *something.*

"Brandon, I want you to do something with your life, all right?" his dad said. His voice was trembling. "I want you to get out of this building and survive and do something worth living for. Do you understand?"

"Stop it!" Brandon cried. "Stop talking like that!"

"Brandon—"

"No!" Brandon told him. "No, we're a team. *I need you.*"

"No you don't," his dad told him. "You're strong, Brandon. You make good decisions."

Brandon sobbed. "But I *don't.* I'm always making mistakes. I got suspended from school. I ran away from you this morning."

"I'm glad you did, Brandon. If you hadn't gone off on your own, you'd be trapped up here with me right now."

"I wish I was!" Brandon told him.

"No you don't, Brandon."

But he did. Brandon wished he was with his father, even if the floors were buckling and the fire was spreading and they couldn't breathe. Even if his dad was dying. Brandon would rather die with his dad than live alone.

"We survive *together.* That's what you always say," Brandon said. He couldn't see for his tears. "I can't do this alone."

"Yes you can, Brandon. You're already becoming your own man. You can survive without me."

Brandon put his elbows on the desk and covered his face with one hand. He didn't want to be a man, or make his own decisions, or survive all by himself. He wanted his dad.

"The firemen are going to rescue you," Brandon managed to say. "They're going to make it up to the 93rd floor and put out the fire and come get you."

But even as he said it, Brandon knew it wasn't true. They both did. Brandon hadn't even seen any firemen yet.

"Brandon, is that man still with you? The one you were with?"

"Richard," Brandon said. He sniffed. "Yes."

"Tell him I need to talk to him."

Brandon didn't want to let his father go, but he was crying so hard now he could barely talk. He held the phone out to Richard but couldn't even say why.

Richard understood. He hung up the phone he'd been using to try to get through to his own family and took the receiver.

"This is Richard," he said into the phone.

Brandon couldn't hear what his father was saying, but Richard nodded.

"I'll make sure he's safe," Richard said.

Brandon choked back another sob. This was all so stupid! His dad wasn't going to die. *He couldn't.* This wasn't how people died. People didn't die on sunny September mornings, going to work like they did every other day of their lives. People died when they were old, in hospital beds or old folks' homes.

Brandon's father kept talking. Richard closed his eyes and lowered his head.

"I understand," Richard said at last. "I will. I promise."

Richard held the phone back out to Brandon. "He needs to talk to you again," he said.

Brandon took the phone, holding onto it with both hands like it was the most precious thing in the world.

"Brandon," his father said, his voice faint. "I want you to promise to stay with Richard. At least for a few days, until he can figure things out."

"No!" Brandon said, tears streaming down his face. "I want to stay with you!"

"Do what I tell you, Brandon. Promise me."

Brandon could only blubber.

"Brandon, I love you," his father told him. "And I'm proud of you. I always have been. I want you to know that. I know it hasn't been easy since your mother died—"

"No, I know," Brandon said. "I'm sorry, Dad. You were great. I'm sorry I made things harder."

His dad didn't answer back.

"Dad?"

There was no voice on the other end of the line. Just dead air.

Brandon hung up and dialed again, but he couldn't get through.

The number was no longer in service.

RESHMINA

MOVING FORWARD

"Ha-*ha!*" the guard cried, leaping through the flowers.

Reshmina threw her hands over her head and cowered, but nothing happened. When she peeked out, she saw the guard through the flowers, a few meters away. He wasn't looking in her direction at all. That snake had been lying about seeing her, trying to get her to reveal herself!

Reshmina stayed low and quiet, watching the guard. He was Afghan and young. Older than her, but not by much. A teenager. He was gangly and thin, with a wisp of beard on his chin.

A boy-man, Reshmina thought. Like the ANA soldiers she'd seen in the village.

This couldn't have been his field, then. He was

guarding it for someone else. For the Taliban? It could be. This was the kind of job they might have Pasoon doing soon.

"Is somebody there?" the boy called again. This time Reshmina heard the fear in his voice. He was just as scared as she was. Reshmina almost felt sorry for him. He was no villain. Just a boy who needed a job.

But he still had a gun, and his job was to shoot her if he caught her.

If I could only go back in time, Reshmina thought. *Just go back in time ten minutes. Make a different decision that would erase this moment.* But was ten minutes enough? How far did she have to go back to avoid the situation she found herself in? Back to the decision to wrestle her brother for the rifle? To follow him from their home? All the way back to the decision to bring the American soldier into her house?

What if every path she chose was the wrong one?

The guard was getting closer. Right or wrong, Reshmina had to make a decision, and fast.

Reshmina picked up a rock from the ground and, when the boy's head was turned, she took a deep breath and threw it across the canyon. It clattered against the steep rock wall on the other side, and the boy spun and fired his rifle.

Ka-tung-ka-tung-ka-tung!

The echo in the little canyon was explosive,

overwhelming. Reshmina put her hands over her ears and ran in a crouch in the opposite direction. Poppies parted and flattened as she ran. Would the guard turn and see her? Shoot her?

Suddenly Reshmina was at the side of the field, in the narrow space next to the canyon wall where no poppies grew. She threw herself to the ground and curled into a ball. She tried to listen, but her heart thundered in her chest and her ears rang from the gunshots.

The boy didn't come, and she couldn't hear what he was doing. She couldn't wait for him to find her. Reshmina looked around and saw she was sitting on a thin, sloping path that ran along the edge of the poppy field. If she followed the path one way, she'd come out where she started. If she went the other way, she would come out where the boy had been leaning against the rock.

Reshmina stood in a crouch again and moved toward where the boy had first been standing guard.

She got to the rock, but the boy hadn't returned. Reshmina chanced a peek over the top of the poppies and saw him on the other side of the canyon, where she'd thrown the rock. He held his rifle at the ready with tight white knuckles. He looked back and forth nervously, sweat beading on his forehead. The boy frowned when he couldn't find anything, then looked back across the poppy field, to where Reshmina had run. He must have seen the path she'd cut through the poppies, because he moved quickly in that direction to investigate.

Reshmina didn't wait to see what happened next. She slipped around the rock and followed the path out of the little canyon. When she was finally out of sight, she ran—ran harder and faster than she had ever run before. Up a ridge she went, slipping and sliding on the loose rocks. Then down into another dip in the peaks, stumbling and cutting herself on rocks and scrub brush. She couldn't slow down. Not until she had put as much distance as she could between herself and the boy with the gun.

At last Reshmina came to a gap in the peaks, and she had to stop. She was out of breath, and her arms and legs were shaking too much.

Reshmina collapsed against a rock and cried. She cried for herself, out of fear and exhaustion. She cried for her family, who had no idea of the terror that was headed their way. She cried for Pasoon, who was lost and gone to her forever. And the worst of it—the absolute worst— was that every single thing that wore her down now, every single cut and bruise that stung her skin, every loss and betrayal that made her sob, all of it was her fault.

It was all because Reshmina had tried to give refuge to a man who asked for help.

Reshmina wiped her eyes with her headscarf and looked out at the view. To the north and the east, beyond the white-capped mountains, was Pakistan. To the west lay the familiar river valley of her home, the houses of her village climbing up into the hills like giant stairs. Reshmina sagged. She had traveled so far in a day, and yet had gone almost nowhere at all. And now she wasn't sure she could go on. That she *should* go on.

Why keep trying when every decision she made was the wrong one?

A small pebble skittered down a steep hill a few meters away, as though something had knocked it loose. Reshmina's eyes flashed to it. She caught the slightest of movements, as though the rocks themselves were alive, but nothing was there.

Then she saw it.

Reshmina gasped quietly. Camouflaged against the rocks was a snow leopard. And it was looking right at her.

The big cat was light gray and brown with black spots. Reshmina would never have seen it if the rocks under its feet hadn't shifted as it snuck by. It wasn't hunting her, she was sure. Snow leopards might take a sheep or goat from the village every now and then, but they never attacked people.

Reshmina's heart raced all the same. It was incredibly rare to see a snow leopard. It felt almost magical to come face-to-face with one here, now, in this remote, inaccessible place.

The snow leopard held its long tail rigid and stared back at her, its pale eyes flashing in the shadowy light. Reshmina's skin tingled, and energy coursed through her. It was almost as though she could feel the leopard's strength in herself. As though they were two creatures who lived outside the bounds of society, beyond the reach of the rest of the world. She breathed in and out, matching the slow, powerful rise and fall of the snow leopard's chest.

Poom.

The tiny echo of an explosion somewhere far away made them both flinch. Reshmina instinctively looked over her shoulder, toward the sound. When she looked back, the snow leopard was already darting off, around the other side of the mountain.

"Safe travels, leopard," Reshmina whispered. "Peace be upon you."

The snow leopard was gone, but the humming, rippling strength of it remained. Reshmina's long black hair, free of her headscarf, blew around her. She felt a power, a purpose, that she had never felt before.

That morning—before the Americans, before the battle, before Taz, before *everything*—Reshmina and Pasoon had laughed and played like they did when they were children. Reshmina had wanted to capture that moment in amber, to preserve it like a fossil. She hadn't wanted a thing in her life to ever change again. But insects trapped in amber, fossils preserved in stone, those things were *dead*. Forever stuck in the past.

And the Kochi—Reshmina had longed for their fairy-tale life, riding camels through mountain passes and trading food and stories around the campfires of a hundred different villages and towns. But as idyllic as that sounded, Reshmina didn't want to be a Kochi either. They had been living the same lives, uninterrupted and unchanged, for thousands of years. Every generation the same as the last. There was no way up, and no way out.

Moving forward was scary. Sometimes you made mistakes. Sometimes you took the wrong path. And sometimes, even when you took the *right* path, things could go wrong. But Reshmina realized that she wanted—*needed*—to keep moving forward, no matter what.

It *was* her fault that her family was in danger. It *was* her fault that Pasoon had chosen today to leave and join the Taliban. If she had chosen revenge over refuge with Taz, she and Pasoon would still be home right now, living their normal lives.

But sometimes what was right and what was easy were two different things.

With renewed strength in her heart, Reshmina drew her scarf up around her head and started down the mountain toward her village.

BRANDON

NEW YORK'S BRAVEST

Brandon almost tripped on a high-heeled shoe. The World Trade Center stairs were littered with uncomfortable work shoes, hand-held radios that got no reception, bulky laptop computers, jackets—anything people had decided they were tired of carrying or wearing after an hour of walking down the stairs. It made the going even slower to dodge all the castoffs.

The crowd stopped moving again, trapped for long minutes between the 17th and 16th floors. A few steps ahead of Brandon and Richard, a woman began to sob quietly, and another woman took her hand and squeezed it.

Brandon felt his own tears coming back. How was it possible that he might never see his dad again, when just that morning they'd been eating breakfast together?

Brushing their teeth together? Riding the train together?

Richard put a hand on his shoulder. "Hey, kid," he said quietly. "You're going to be all right."

Brandon shook his head. How was he going to be all right? How was anything ever going to be all right ever again?

"I didn't say I loved him," Brandon said. The tears came harder now, and he turned toward the wall to hide his face. "He told me he loved me, and I never said it back, and now he's—"

Brandon didn't want to finish. Didn't want to say it out loud.

Now he's going to die.

Richard pulled Brandon into a hug. "He knows, kid. Trust me. He knows. And as much as he loves you, he's happier you're down here than up there with him."

Brandon cried into Richard's shirt until they had to take another step. He sniffed and rubbed his eyes. "What am I going to do now? Where am I going to live?"

"Your dad said his parents live in Honduras."

"Yeah, but I can't go live in another country," Brandon said. "I live here!"

"What about your mom's parents?" Richard asked.

"They're really old, and they live in Idaho," Brandon explained. "I never see them. I barely know them. I don't want to go live with strangers. This is where I live. Where I go to school. New York City is my home."

They took another step down and waited again.

"If my mom and dad are both gone—" Brandon swallowed down another sob. "If my mom and dad are gone, that makes me an orphan, right? Will I go into a foster home?"

"It's too soon to worry about any of that," Richard told him. "We gotta worry about getting out of here first, okay? And maybe your dad will make it out after all."

Brandon sniffed and nodded, but he knew that wasn't happening. They both did.

Brandon heard cheering from below, and someone called out, "Stay to the right! Firefighters coming up!"

Firefighters? At last! Brandon felt a surge of hope, and he and Richard stepped aside with the others.

The first man from the New York Fire Department came huffing up the stairs. He was white, with brown hair and bright blue eyes, and he wore a big, bulky black jacket with fluorescent yellow bands and matching long pants and heavy boots. A tall black helmet sat on his head, and he carried a hatchet in one hand and a shovel in the other. On his back was a giant oxygen tank. The firefighter behind him was Black, with broad shoulders and stubble on his face. He was just as loaded down, carrying a pickax and a huge length of white canvas water hose.

Brandon couldn't believe how much gear they were wearing and carrying. It had to be fifty pounds' worth of stuff, and Brandon was tired just walking *down* seventy-five flights. These guys had to go *up* that far, hauling all that equipment.

The people along the wall burst into spontaneous applause for the rescuers, and the firefighters stopped for a moment to wave with gratitude and catch their breath. People patted them on the shoulders and thanked them.

"God bless you," a woman said, giving the fire-fighter next to her a hug.

People handed them the plastic water bottles they'd been given upstairs, and the firefighters guzzled them gratefully.

"Don't worry, the fire's far above you," the lead fire-man told Brandon as he passed. "Keep going. It's safe downstairs."

"There's fire all over the 93rd floor," Brandon told them. "We saw it. You have to get up there. My dad's trapped on the top floor, and the smoke is really bad."

The fireman nodded. He and his partner were grim and stone-faced, as were the firefighters behind them, no doubt thinking about the long, grueling climb ahead of them. And they were only at the 16th floor.

Brandon, Richard, and everyone else escaping the building kept walking along just one side of the stairs. More and more firefighters passed them, and even though it slowed his escape, Brandon was glad to see them keep coming. Going up, toward the trouble, while everybody else went down.

Just after the 12th-floor landing, Brandon heard a man's voice on a bullhorn blasting up the stairwell. "Stay calm and keep walking down in an orderly fashion!" he called. Then, inexplicably, he started singing "God Bless America."

Richard and Brandon looked at each other.

"I was always more partial to 'This Land Is Your Land,'" Richard said. "A little less . . . bombastic."

Brandon didn't care what song the man sang. He just wanted to get out of this stairwell.

When they reached the 11th floor, Richard and Brandon finally saw the man who'd been serenading them. He was a big white security guard, wearing khaki slacks and a blue jacket with a WORLD TRADE CENTER patch on it. "This is a day you'll never forget!" he told them. "This is a day that will go down in history!"

"Why?" Brandon asked. "What's going on?"

"They flew a plane into the Pentagon too," the security guard told them.

There were gasps up and down the stairs.

"Who did?" Richard asked.

"Somebody who's about to get their butts kicked by the US of A!" the security guard told them.

Brandon frowned. So the security guard didn't know who'd done it. Nobody knew. All they knew was that somebody was flying planes into buildings in America, and for some reason they'd chosen the very building Brandon's dad worked in. The building where Brandon just happened to be that day because he was suspended from school. If only he could go back in time and not punch Stuart Pendleton in the nose! But he had, and here he was. Now he just had to move forward. And he would, if people would just move forward on the stairs!

Down they went, step by maddeningly slow step. Past the 10th floor. Then the 9th. More and more people squeezed into the stairwells at every level. They couldn't be office workers from those floors, Brandon thought. Those people would have been out of the building long ago. They must be people from other stairwells, looking for a faster route down, the way he and Richard had. But there was no faster route now.

The new people forced their way into the line where there wasn't space, and suddenly everybody was pushing forward. But there wasn't anywhere to go. The woman behind Brandon smushed right up against him, pressing him into the back of the man in front of him on the stairs.

"Hey! Quit shoving!" the man cried.

"I can't help it!" Brandon told him.

The mob kept surging forward, and Brandon was crushed between the woman behind him and the man in front of him. He started to panic—he couldn't see, couldn't move, couldn't breathe—and then all at once his feet were lifted off the ground, and he was being swept forward against his will.

"Richard!" Brandon cried, turning his head around. "Help!"

"Watch the kid! Watch the kid!" Richard called out. He was already three steps behind Brandon. Richard reached out through the bodies, and Brandon stretched out a hand to try to grab him, but they were too far away from each other. A moment later Richard disappeared, and Brandon was on his own again, swept down the stairs by a river of pressing bodies.

RESHMINA

UNDER THE BURQA

Reshmina ran up the steps of her village, taking them two at a time. She didn't see any American soldiers, or any Taliban. Not yet. Was she in time?

Reshmina burst through the front door of her house. "Mor! Baba!" she cried. Two Afghan men with rifles were sitting just inside the door, and Reshmina jumped back. Who were they? Why were they here?

Marzia and Mor came in from the women's room.

"Reshmina, it's all right!" Marzia told her. "The village sent them to guard us and the American."

So Taz was still here! That meant Baba wasn't back from the ANA base yet.

"Where have you been, Reshmina?" Mor demanded.

"Where did you get those scratches? Those bruises? You're filthy!"

"The Taliban are coming!" Reshmina cried. "They know the American is here! Pasoon told them!"

The guards jumped to their feet, their faces a mix of shock and horror.

Anaa came into the front room with Zahir in her arms. She had heard everything. "Go and warn the others in the village," she told the guards. "Tell them they must get to safety."

"Where?" one of the men said. "What place is safe?"

Reshmina grabbed her mother's arm. "Mor, let's take everything we can and leave the village. Let's go to Kabul."

"*Go to Kabul?*" Mor said. "You foolish girl. That must be three hundred kilometers! It would take us days to walk there, and days to come back!"

"I mean go and never come back," Reshmina said. She was tired of standing still. She wasn't sure the capital city was the right place to go, but it had to be better than their village. "We'll live in Kabul forever."

Mor looked at her like she'd lost her mind. "Without land to farm? Without a place to live? Nonsense."

"Anaa still has family there, don't you?" Reshmina asked her grandmother. "There must be someone. A nephew. A distant cousin."

"Child—" Anaa said in that infuriating tone adults used when they were going to dismiss your idea out of hand.

Anger flared in Reshmina. It was just like her mother to say no, but Anaa too? Why couldn't they leave this village and the Taliban behind and never come back? Move forward, even if it was hard?

"Now is not the time, Mina-jan," Anaa told her. "We need a more immediate solution. Many people are in danger."

Reshmina huffed, but her grandmother was right. Running away wouldn't save the rest of the village. But where could you hide an entire village?

Hide.

Reshmina remembered playing hide-and-seek with Pasoon when they were young, and suddenly she had the answer.

"The caves!" Reshmina said. "The caves beneath the village! We can hide there!"

"Stay and watch the American," one of the guards told the other. "I'll go tell the others."

The guard hurried off. Mor and Marzia began gathering things to take with them, and Reshmina followed Anaa and Zahir into the women's room.

Taz still lay on the mat, sleeping. Reshmina was relieved to see him alive. But he wouldn't be for very long if they didn't move. None of them would be.

Reshmina dropped to her knees next to Taz. Anaa had wrapped wet cloths around his wounds, but fresh blood had already soaked through some of the bandages. Anaa had also wiped away the black marks on his face from the explosion, but the skin around his eyes was still bright red and raw.

"Taz," she said. "Taz, wake up. We have to go. The Taliban are coming."

Taz instantly jerked awake. "What? Where? Are they here?"

"No, not yet. But they will be soon. I'm sorry, but we must move."

"Reshmina," Taz said, anguish in his voice as he blinked, "I still can't see!"

"I will lead you," Reshmina told him. "Follow my voice, like before."

Pakow. Pakow.

They heard shots in the distance. Reshmina knew what that meant.

The Taliban were almost here.

The guard rushed in from the other room. "We have to go!" he cried. The guard helped Taz to his feet. Reshmina frowned. How were they going to hide Taz until they got him into the caves?

Anaa was one step ahead of her. She came into the room with an old blue burqa, the kind of garment women had been forced to wear outside during the rule of the Taliban. It was a robe that covered every inch of a woman's body, from head to foot, with a small mesh window to see out of. Some women still wore them by choice, but not Reshmina's mother or grandmother.

"Put this on him, quickly," Anaa said.

The guard helped Taz into the burqa. It hid his head and his shape, but the material only came down to his ankles. Reshmina just had to hope the Taliban wouldn't notice that the "woman" under this burqa was wearing American army boots.

"Come," Reshmina said. "We must hurry." The guard took Taz's elbow and led him to the front room and out the door. Reshmina, Marzia, and Anaa followed, along with Mor, who carried Zahir.

The steps down through the village were already crowded with people who'd been warned by the other guard. They carried children, chickens, bundles of clothing, and treasured possessions. Anything of value they could take with them.

Reshmina's family went slowly, staying with Taz and the guard. As they descended, more and more people joined them on the twisting switchback stairs that led down through the gray-and-brown stone walls of the village.

Higher above them, toward the top of the village, something exploded—*P-TOOM*—and Reshmina froze in fear. She turned to see the hilltop glow orange with flame. There were more cries, and more gunfire. The Taliban had arrived.

THUMP-THUMP-THUMP-THUMP. An Apache helicopter thundered by right overhead, and Reshmina ducked instinctively.

"That's my people!" Taz cried, recognizing the sound of the helicopter.

Reshmina's heart sank. Now the Americans were here too! That was good in one way: The Americans would keep the Taliban busy. But in another way it was very, very bad.

Now the village was a war zone.

Taz stopped in the middle of the stairs. "Maybe we can just flag them down, let them know where I am!"

PERRRT! PERRRRRRT! the helicopter's machine gun erupted, and something exploded in the village with a *BOOM.*

"No, not now," Reshmina told him.

"Nope! Not now!" Taz agreed, letting them hurry him along.

Reshmina suddenly heard the familiar sound of a missile hissing across the valley and turned to look. The villagers all around her knew the sound too, and they ducked, giving Reshmina a clear view of the thing as it streaked across the valley.

Shhhhh-THOOM!

The missile slammed into a house on the hillside, and the building exploded.

"No!" Reshmina cried.

"Reshmina, what is it? What's happened?" Taz asked her.

Reshmina couldn't answer. Couldn't find the words.

The rocket had just destroyed Reshmina's home.

BRANDON

DON'T LOOK

Brandon kicked and fought, trying to get free of the people pressing in on him from all sides.

"Help!" he cried. "I can't breathe! Please!"

More people cried out, and from below, someone shouted, "Back it up! Back it up!"

And then, mercifully, the people on the stairs did exactly that. The lady behind Brandon took a step back up, and that was enough to stop pushing him into the man in front of him. Brandon's feet landed back on the stairs, and he grabbed the handrail as he fought to catch his breath.

"Coming through!" Richard cried somewhere up the stairs above Brandon. "I'm trying to get to my kid! Please!" The people on the stairs parted, and then Richard was there, holding Brandon while they both wept tears of exhaustion and relief.

"I just about lost you back there," Richard said. "Promised your dad I wouldn't do that."

Brandon nodded, his head still buried in Richard's chest. He'd been telling the truth when he'd told his dad he couldn't do this alone. He couldn't survive without Richard either.

"How did things clear up?" Brandon asked.

"The man with the bullhorn, upstairs. When he saw what was happening, he made people stop coming down for a minute. Gave us room to spread out again."

Thank goodness for the man with the bullhorn, Brandon thought.

"I'm sorry I crushed you," the woman behind Brandon told him. "I couldn't help it."

Brandon understood. So did the man in front of him when Brandon apologized for kicking him. "For what it's worth," the man said, "I was freaking out too."

There were no stair exits at floors 8, 7, and 6, which made Brandon feel even more claustrophobic. What if people started pushing forward again? He couldn't get out of the stairwell now if he wanted to. But they were *so close*. Just five more floors to go!

At last the stairwell dead-ended at a doorway on the second floor. There was a palpable sense of excitement from the people around Brandon as they all filed into a short, dark passageway. The crowd squeezed in more tightly again.

"Hey, watch the kid, watch the kid!" Richard said, keeping his hand on Brandon's shoulder.

Things stayed tight but didn't get out of control. As they inched forward, Brandon's feet splashed through water, and he coughed from the dust and smoke in the air. If he didn't know better, Brandon would have thought they were going *toward* the trouble, not away from it.

And then, at last, more than an hour after the first plane had hit the North Tower, Richard and Brandon stepped out into the tall, open-air mezzanine above the lobby. It was the same half floor Brandon had seen above him when he'd gotten his ID that morning, and he blinked in the bright, sudden sunlight coming in through the floor-to-ceiling windows.

"Keep moving!" a Port Authority policeman told them.

There were a bunch of Port Authority officers here on the mezzanine, all lined up with their backs to the windows. The Port Authority were the people who managed all the subways and tunnels and bridges and seaports in New York and New Jersey. They ran the World Trade Center too.

There were escalators right in front of Brandon that would take him straight down to the lobby and out the front doors onto the street. But the Port Authority police were directing everybody *away* from the escalators, toward a set of stairs on the far wall. Brandon was confused. Why couldn't they just go down the escalators? That was the quickest way out of the building. Even if the escalators weren't working, they could use them as stairs. Why send everybody all the way around?

Brandon did as he was told and didn't ask questions, and Richard followed suit.

As they shuffled along, Brandon realized why there were Port Authority officers lining the windows. There was something out there they didn't want anybody to see. There weren't enough of them to completely block the view though, and Brandon snuck a look.

He gasped at what he saw. Out on the plaza between the North Tower and the South Tower were bodies. And parts of bodies. Broken, bloody things too awful to think about. Brandon didn't want to look, but he couldn't look away either. It was like a horror movie. It couldn't be real. *How could what he was looking at be real?*

Thousands of sheets of paper fell like snow around the bodies, and broken glass and twisted metal were everywhere. While Brandon watched, a piece of metal crashed into the plaza—*SHANG!*—and Brandon flinched. The big beam was immediately followed by something white and blue and brown plummeting down from above, and it hit the ground with a sickening *THUMP.*

Brandon put his hands to his mouth and turned away. He had just seen a human being hit the ground from very high up.

"Keep moving," a Port Authority policewoman said, "and don't look down into the lobby!"

Brandon looked down into the lobby.

It was even worse than the plaza. The big, beautiful lobby where Brandon had been that morning was where the emergency responders had decided to take all the injured and burned people. Dozens, *hundreds* of bodies were lined up in rows across the floor. Some of them had missing limbs. Others had open wounds. Paramedics moved among the burned, broken, and dying people, doing what they could. Dust and debris were everywhere. The elevator shafts in the center of the lobby were twisted and mangled where cars had fallen, and there was a dull, ammonia-like taste in the air, like the way hospitals smelled.

"Don't look! Keep moving!" the Port Authority police told them.

Brandon kept moving, but he kept looking too. He should have been sick. He should have been screaming. But it was all so surreal. So impossible. He felt like a character in a movie, walking through a nightmare that couldn't be real.

Their scenic tour through hell came to an end on the other side of the mezzanine. A white Port Authority policewoman with her brown hair in a ponytail pointed them toward another staircase.

"Wait, doesn't this go into the basement?" Richard asked. "Why can't we just go outside?"

"We can't take you out through the lobby, it's too full of injured people," the policewoman said. "And it's dangerous right outside the building."

Brandon knew why. Outside through the window he could still hear what sounded like pebbles and stones raining down on the concrete plaza. But he knew they weren't pebbles and stones. They were bits of building and glass windows. And people.

"Keep going," the policewoman told them. "You'll come up on the other side of the plaza, away from all this."

"*What if the building comes down on top of us?*" a hysterical man asked.

The policewoman shook her head. "It's a steel structure. No way it's coming down. Go on—trust me, you'll be safer down there."

Brandon hated to go into another stairwell. He almost balked, almost backed out, but he knew there was no way out across that plaza. Not with all that stuff raining down from above. They'd just as likely be killed by a falling piece of metal or . . . well, he didn't like to think about what else.

Brandon took a deep breath and followed Richard and the others down the stairs. This wasn't a tight stairwell like before. This was a bigger set of stairs, and everyone was at last able to spread out and move at their own pace. Brandon let out a sigh of relief, even though they were still inside the building. It finally felt like he had room to breathe.

Richard and Brandon went down two floors of steps to a bank of revolving doors that had been opened up so they could pass straight through without spinning them. Just beyond that was a larger public space, and suddenly Brandon recognized where they were.

They were back where he'd started his day, in the underground mall beneath the World Trade Center.

RESHMINA

DEATH CALLS

Reshmina stood still, staring at the place where her house had been. People from her village flowed around her like water around a rock in the river. She couldn't even see over their heads anymore, but she could see the black-and-gray plume of smoke as it rose into the air.

Her house. The place where she and her family had been standing just minutes ago was gone. Destroyed. Blasted into bits. The house where she had been born. The house where she had spent every day and night of her life.

Not just her house. Her *home*. The place she always came back to.

Her home was no more.

"Reshmina!" her mother cried. "Reshmina, move! We have to get to the caves!"

"Our house, Mor," Reshmina said quietly. "Our home. They blew it up."

"They'll blow us up too if we don't go!" her mother told her. "We'll find a new place to live, Reshmina. Now please come!"

PAK-PAK-PAK-PAK!

T-koom. T-koom. T-koom.

An assault rifle barked, and another fired back. The villagers screamed. The Taliban and the Americans were both in the village now, and fighting each other. Nobody was safe.

What have I done? Reshmina thought.

Her mother had been right. She had brought death to them all.

Still in a daze, she caught up to Taz and the guard.

"Is everything all right?" Taz asked from inside the burqa. "Where's Reshmina? Is she all right?"

"I'm here," Reshmina said. "They blew up my house with a rocket."

"Who blew up your house? Not the Americans," he said defensively. "Not if your dad told them I was somewhere in the village. They would never fire a missile into the village if they thought I was here."

The Taliban, then. They had blown up her house, trying to get at the Americans. The Americans who shouldn't have been there in the first place.

Not just *any* Americans, Reshmina realized. One in

particular. The Taliban had fired at her house on purpose because Pasoon had told them Taz was there.

Reshmina felt like she was sinking. Like her body was still standing, still moving down the steps, but her *spirit* was draining out of her, leaving her hollow and empty inside. That her brother had finally gone to join the Taliban shouldn't have surprised her. All the boys did eventually. That was the path Pasoon had been headed down, long before today.

But to have pointed out his *own home* to them, with his own mother and grandmother and brother and sister in it, knowing the Taliban would shoot a missile at it? How could the brother she loved have been so heartless? So evil?

PAK-PAK-PAK-PAK!

Bullets hit the wall beside them, spraying them with bits of concrete and rock. They all ducked, and Reshmina scanned the rooftops. There—a Taliban fighter with an AK-47!

The guard next to Taz whipped the rifle off his shoulder and shot back.

PAKOW. PAKOW.

PAK-PAK-PAK!

Taliban bullets struck the guard, and he fell to the ground, dead. Reshmina screamed. She put her hands over her head, bracing for the bullets she knew were coming for her next, but then—

T-koom. T-koom. T-koom.

—an American soldier on a nearby rooftop fired back, and the Taliban fighter fell.

Reshmina started to call out to the American soldier, to tell him Taz was with them. But at the same moment, from the other side of the steps, came the sound of another AK-47. *PAK-PAK-PAK.* The American soldier on the rooftop immediately took cover and traded bullets with his unseen attacker above the line of frightened villagers heading down the stairs.

"Come! Follow my voice! Hurry!" Reshmina yelled to Taz. Their only hope was to make it to the safety of the caves, and then wait out the fight.

K-THOOM! K-THOOM! K-THOOM!

Huge blasts rocked the village above them, and three more houses exploded in clouds of rock and splinter. Reshmina didn't know if it was Taliban RPGs or the American helicopter. Or both.

"Don't look! Go! Go!" an elderly man behind them cried.

People bottlenecked at the bottom of the steps, but soon the survivors were out onto the small path that led along the river. A few people ran in the direction of Asadabad, just trying to get as far away as quickly as possible, but more of the villagers followed Reshmina and her family down toward the caves. The entrance was small, and overgrown with brush, but they were all able to squeeze through. Even Taz.

And then, at last, they were in the dark, ancient caves underneath the village.

BRANDON

BUGS BUNNY AND DESIGNER JEANS

Sprinklers rained down from the ceiling of the underground mall, and in seconds Brandon was soaked through to the skin.

He squinted, trying to see in the rain and the darkness. There were burn marks around the blown-out elevator doors by the stairs, as though giant balls of flame had blasted down all the way from above. There was no fire that Brandon could see, but the sprinklers still ran. The water on the floor was ankle deep.

Port Authority and New York City police guided people toward the exit to Church Street on the other side of the mall. Brandon didn't need directions. He knew this mall like he knew his own neighborhood. There was the familiar coffee shop to his left and the Banana Republic just ahead on the right. Beyond that would be the Gap, and the Speedo store where Brandon liked to laugh at the male mannequins in their skimpy bathing suits. Farther along, he knew, was the Duane Reade where he and his father bought cough medicine and snacks, and a Sbarro where they sometimes grabbed a quick slice of pizza before heading home.

"Keep moving!" a policeman called through a bullhorn.

The mall looked very different than it had that morning. The main hallway was like a gushing aqueduct during a storm, but the electricity was still on in the stores. TVs ran, music played, and lights glowed. But there was no one there. No clerks, no salespeople, no cooks, no customers.

For the first time in Brandon's life, the mall felt incredibly garish. The lights were too bright, the music too happy. And the things for sale: Designer jeans. LEGO sets and plastic dinosaurs. Sunglasses and necklaces and greeting cards and remote-controlled cars. How could anybody care about all that stuff? How could any of that matter when there were people flying planes into buildings? When there were people trapped and burned and broken and jumping and dying?

How could any of this ever matter again after what Brandon had seen?

A woman near them stopped and cried, and Richard put an arm around her shoulder.

"Come on. We gotta go," he told her. "It's going to be okay."

They came to an intersection. To the right were more shops. To the left, past the Borders bookstore, were stairs down to the subway and the escalator up to Church Street. Straight ahead of them was the Warner Bros. Store, with its Bugs Bunny and Daffy Duck statues outside the entrance.

How many afternoons had Brandon and his dad spent watching Batman and Superman and Looney Tunes cartoons? They were both big fans, and they loved going in the Warner Bros. Store and looking at all the super-hero T-shirts and stuffed cartoon animals and movie posters.

All of it was drowning in sprinklers now.

As the water poured down, Brandon pictured his dad trapped up in Windows on the World. Smoke pouring in, and no water to put out the fire climbing up from below.

"Brandon, we have to go," Richard told him. "We're almost out."

"They have phones in the store," Brandon said, wiping his eyes. "We could try my dad again."

"Not exactly the best place to stop," Richard said, squinting up into the water coming down from the sprinklers. "Come on. We'll call from a pay phone out on the street."

The ground underneath Brandon's feet suddenly began to vibrate, and Brandon threw his arms out to steady himself. It felt like a subway car rattling by beneath them.

But this was no subway car. The rumbling grew and grew, and Brandon and Richard just had time to look at each other in horror before something exploded above and behind them. It was like the whole mall collapsed in on them at once, and with a roar like a garbage truck, a blast of smoke and dust lifted Brandon off his feet and hurled him into darkness.

RESHMINA

OLD TIRES AND RPG LAUNCHERS

It was cool and damp and dark inside the cave, and eerily quiet. Reshmina could still hear the pops and booms of guns above, but they were muted here. Muffled by the meters of rock that Reshmina hoped would keep them safe until the battle was over.

Reshmina took a step forward and banged her shin on something metal. She yelped in pain.

"What is it?" Taz asked. "What's wrong?"

Reshmina forgot he still couldn't see. "We're in a cave now. We're safe," she told him. "But it's dark. I ran into something."

"Here—use my flashlight," Taz said.

She heard the rip of Velcro, and Taz fumbled to lift the burqa he wore.

"Here, I think we can liberate him now," Anaa

said, and she helped Taz out of the burqa.

Reshmina took the flashlight and clicked it on. The cave was smaller than she remembered. But the cave *would* have looked bigger to her back then, she realized. The last time she'd been here it had just been her and Pasoon and a few other kids, playing hide-and-seek. Now she was taller, and a dozen or so families from her village were squeezed inside with her.

"I wish your baba was here," Reshmina's mother said. She had Zahir in one arm and held Marzia's hand with the other. "I hope he's safe."

Reshmina hoped he was too. He had made it to the ANA base, at least, and they had gotten his message to the Americans that Taz was in the village. The soldiers fighting up above them were proof enough of that.

Reshmina used Taz's flashlight to lead Taz and her family to the back of the cave, as far away from the entrance as they could get. The cave was full of rusty old Soviet-era junk they had to step around. Propellers, engine parts, spare tires, electronics with wires sticking out like wild hairs, big pieces of metal from trucks. And parts of old weapons too—the metal bits of rifles, RPG launchers with no rockets, disassembled land mines.

"Be careful!" one of the older men from the village said. "Some of these weapons might explode if you kick them the wrong way!"

Their parents had told them the same thing when they were little, of course. Told them in no uncertain terms *not* to play in the caves beneath the village. That it was too dangerous. All that had done, of course, was make Reshmina and Pasoon and the others want to come down here and explore. Besides, how was it any safer to play aboveground, when there were Americans and Taliban running around shooting at each other?

Reshmina remembered wandering, amazed, through all the old Soviet-era machines. They had been so foreign, so mysterious.

Now they just looked sad.

Taz put his hands out, frowning as he tried to feel what was around him. "I hate being blind," he said.

Reshmina turned off the flashlight, saving the battery. "We're all in the dark," she told him.

"I'm scared of the dark," Taz confessed. "I was lost in the dark once and couldn't see. When I was a boy. It was very scary. I've been afraid of the dark ever since."

Reshmina wasn't afraid of the dark. Lantern fuel was expensive, and they burned the lantern in their house only when they had to. She got up just before dawn every day and went to bed every night after the sun went down. Darkness was just another part of her world. Not something to love or fear. But whatever had happened to Taz as a boy, being in the dark was making him sweat with panic now.

Poom. Poom. Dirt and rock misted down from the cave ceiling as muffled explosions struck nearby.

"M320 grenade launcher," Taz said.

"How do you know?" Reshmina asked.

"The sound. The feel," Taz said. "I've been here a long time."

"How long?" Reshmina asked.

"Ten years, off and on," Taz told her.

"Ten years, and you speak no Pashto?" Reshmina asked.

Taz didn't answer right away. Perhaps he was ashamed. Reshmina would be. After all, *she* had spent the last few years of her life learning English.

"I speak Mandarin Chinese," Taz said.

"You speak Chinese?" Reshmina asked. She couldn't believe it.

"Shì de," Taz said. "Army Special Forces have to learn a second language, and I was taught Mandarin."

"Because so many people in Afghanistan speak Chinese," Reshmina said wryly.

"I guess they figured there was life after Afghanistan," Taz said. From the way he said it, it sounded like Taz wasn't so sure that was true anymore.

The ground and walls shook, and Reshmina felt her insides shake with them. She knew that feeling—a helicopter was flying by.

"Apache," she said.

Taz shook his head. "Sikorsky HH-60 Pave Hawk," he told her. "Modified Black Hawk. Apaches are more like *pppppppp*," he said, blowing out through his lips. "Sixties are more like *ch-ch-ch-ch-ch-ch*. The Sixties are for me, I guess. They're search-and-rescue birds."

All this was for Taz, Reshmina thought. And all because she'd led him back to her house.

Her house that wasn't there anymore.

Toom.

Something big exploded on the ground above the cave, and the interior shook harder than before. A woman cried out as a piece of one of the walls broke off and tumbled down into the metal junk on the floor.

Reshmina watched Taz, who was suddenly alert.

TOOM.

The next explosion was bigger, closer. This one knocked them all to the ground. Reshmina's eyes went wide, and she put her palms against the dirt, as though she could command the earth to stop shaking. It didn't work, and she began to think that coming into the caves was a very, very bad idea.

What if this place became their tomb?

A chunk of the ceiling fell on an old man toward the front of the cave, and the people around him cried out and tried to unbury him.

Taz put his hand to the wall and slowly stood, a look of fear on his face.

"What is it?" Reshmina asked, still on the ground.

"I don't know. It's hard to tell down here. But to shake us like that . . . it feels like Reaper drones. Laser-guided bombs!"

No sooner had Taz said it than—*K-TOOM!*—a bomb hit right on top of the cave, and the whole ceiling fell in.

BRANDON

BLIND

Brandon's eyes fluttered open, but he couldn't see a thing. He was lying on his side in three inches of water, arms and legs splayed out and pieces of metal and wood on top of him. The darkness pressed in on him, like he'd been holding his breath in a pool for too long and the water was trying to push its way in. The air was a solid thing that surrounded him. He couldn't breathe, couldn't hear. He tried to move his arms, but they didn't want to move. His legs were like dead lumps attached to his hips.

Brandon's heart hammered in his chest, and he gasped for air. His mouth and nose were full of dust and little bits of debris, and he coughed and spat and retched until most of it was gone. Slowly, dully, the feeling in his arms and legs came tingling back. But his eyesight didn't.

Panic welled up inside him. *I'm blind*, Brandon thought. *I'm blind and I'm lost and I'm alone and the air is closing in on me and I'm never going to get out of here.*

"Richard?" he called. "Richard? Are you there?"

No one answered, and Brandon sobbed. He couldn't see and his ears were ringing and he was all alone.

"Richard!" he called again. But Richard was gone.

Brandon curled up into a ball and cried. The world had exploded, and now he was totally, utterly alone. All his life, a parent had been there for him. First his mother, who had loved him and laughed with him and cared for him when he was little. He remembered her face—her blonde hair and pale skin and blue eyes—more from photographs now than his own fading memories. But the *idea* of her was still there—a tall, warm, embracing figure who picked him up and sang him lullabies.

When his mother had died, Brandon had thought he couldn't go on. He had stopped talking, stopped caring. Every night he had cried himself to sleep.

It was his father who brought him back. His father, who had probably been losing sleep too, and who might have wanted to withdraw from the world when his wife had died but hadn't, for Brandon's sake. His father who had read comic books with him and taken him to the skate park every weekend. They had been a team.

And now Brandon was alone.

He couldn't do it. He couldn't go on. It would have been better if he had never run away at all and stayed trapped in Windows on the World with his father, with the smoke choking them. He needed his father to make the decisions, to guide him through the danger.

Without his father, Brandon thought, he was better off dead.

But eventually his tears dried and the sprinkler stopped and the ringing in his ears faded, and Brandon was still there. He *wasn't* dead. He was battered and sore, but his head, his face, his arms, his body, his legs and feet—they were all still there, still working. He had little cuts and bruises all over, but he was alive, and in one piece, and he couldn't just lie here in the dark forever. What was it his father had told him?

You're strong, Brandon. You can survive without me.

Brandon *was* strong. And he *had* survived, all by himself. He didn't want to, but he could when he needed to. And he needed to now.

Brandon put a hand down into the water to push himself to his feet and felt the razor-sharp burn of a broken piece of glass cutting into his palm. He pulled back with a hiss and squeezed his hands together. The mall shops all around him must have been destroyed in the blast, which meant there was broken glass and debris everywhere now. He couldn't *see*, and now he was lost in what was left of the underground mall after it had been nuked.

But nuked by what? Had another plane crashed into the plaza above them? Who was doing this? And why? Why hurt and kill all these people?

"Richard?" Brandon called again.

He heard someone moan in response.

Richard! He was alive!

The cut on Brandon's hand still stung, but he had to move. He'd lost the handkerchief Richard had given him, but feeling around in the darkness, he found a shirt from one of the stores. He threw the hanger away and wrapped the wet shirt around his injured hand. He couldn't see the cut, but he knew it must be deep from how much it hurt.

"Richard, I'm coming!" Brandon called.

Richard moaned again, and Brandon put his hands out carefully, trying to feel his way toward the sound without hurting himself again. His left hand found something plastic in a cardboard package, floating by in the ankle-deep water, and as he searched its contours with his fingers, Brandon recognized with a start what it was.

It was the toy Wolverine claws he'd left to buy at Sam Goody that morning.

Brandon blinked in the darkness. It was so strange to finally hold the toy in his hands. *This is why I'm here*, Brandon thought. *This is why I'm not with my dad right now.*

This is why I'm alive.

It was so random. So stupid. So meaningless now, and yet so important at the same time.

Richard moaned again, and Brandon dropped the Wolverine claws and focused. Brandon was here, now, for whatever reason, and so was Richard. And Richard needed his help.

Arms and legs trembling, Brandon put his hands out in front of him again and shuffled forward, sloshing through the water and the rubble. The air in front of him was empty, but he was sure he was going to run into something.

"Richard, say something so I can find you," Brandon said.

"I am here," said a man with a heavy Indian accent.

Brandon's heart sank. It wasn't Richard he'd heard moaning. It was someone else.

"Help me. Please," the man said.

"Keep talking so I can find you," Brandon told the man.

"I'm here. I'm alive," the man said. There were tears in his voice. "I don't know what else to tell you. I'm here, and I'm frightened. I don't know what's going on. The world's gone crazy."

Brandon found the man, and they clasped hands like they were a long-lost father and son, finding each other again after years and years.

"Oh my God, I thought I was dead," the man said. "My name is Pratik."

"I'm Brandon."

"I—I can't see," Pratik said.

"I can't see either," Brandon told him.

"Oh, thank God," Pratik said. "I thought I had been blinded. But if you can't see either, then it's just too dark to see."

Brandon was relieved too. *I'm not blind*, he thought. *Not forever.* The electricity must have gone out, and now there wasn't a hint of light anywhere in the windowless mall.

"What happened?" Pratik asked.

"I don't know," Brandon told him. "Maybe another plane. Are you hurt bad? Can you stand?"

"I think my arm is broken, but I can stand."

"Help," a woman rasped nearby. Somewhere else in the darkness, Brandon heard another person groan.

There had been dozens of people with them down here in the mall, all following the Port Authority's directions to the Church Street exit. Some of them might be dead from the blast, but there had to be other survivors like Brandon and Pratik.

They found the woman, who told them her name was Gayle. She managed to stand and join their human chain, and they shuffled their way through the darkness toward the person who was groaning. *Please let it be*

Richard, Brandon thought. *Please let it be Richard.*

The groaning man couldn't speak. Gayle bent down to examine him with her hands, and she gasped and stood.

"We have to leave him," she said.

"Why? What is it?" Brandon asked, afraid it was Richard.

"I'm not sure he's even still alive" was all Gayle would say.

They heard something rattle and fall nearby, and Pratik turned.

"No, wait—" Brandon said. He bent down to check on the wounded man. "I have to know if it's Richard."

"Stay away from his stomach," Gayle told him, her voice queasy.

Brandon's hands found the man's shoulders first, and then his suspenders. Richard had been wearing suspenders! *Please no, please no*, Brandon said to himself.

His hands fumbled for the man's face, and he felt smooth, shaved skin. Brandon cried tears of relief. This couldn't be him. *Richard had a beard.* Brandon felt a pang of guilt for feeling relieved when this man was dying—maybe even dead already—but he couldn't help being grateful.

"I'm sorry," Brandon whispered to the dying man.

Brandon stood, and he and Pratik and Gayle listened again for a groan or a voice in the darkness.

"If you are hurt or trapped and can hear my voice, make any noise you can so we can find you," Pratik called out.

No one answered.

"I think we should go," said Gayle. "It's hard to breathe, and we don't even know which way is out."

"Wait, please," Brandon said. "My friend is still down here somewhere."

"I'm sorry, boy," said Pratik. "But if we haven't heard him by now—"

"Just let me look a little more," Brandon told him. He couldn't leave Richard behind. Not after all they'd been through together.

"Richard?" Brandon called. "Richard!"

Long moments went by, and Brandon could sense the other two survivors growing restless. They wanted to get out of here. He did too.

Brandon pulled the human chain farther into the darkness, desperate to find his friend.

"Richard!" he cried.

Then, softly, Brandon thought he heard something. Was that . . . *singing*? Brandon's ears were still buzzing. Maybe they were playing tricks on him. But no, the others stopped to listen too.

"Richard?" Brandon called.

There was no answer. Just the indistinct hum of a tune.

"I think it's coming from this way," Gayle said, pulling them gently in the dark.

Faintly, almost no more than a whisper, came the words to a familiar song:

This land is your land, this land is my land,
From California, to the New York island—

Brandon gasped. It was Richard!

RESHMINA

MOMARDENE AFGHANE

Reshmina woke to the sound of singing.

We are Afghan people
We are Afghans of the mountains

It was pitch-black and Reshmina couldn't see, but she would know the sound of her grandmother's voice anywhere. The song she was singing, "Momardene Afghane," was one of Anaa's favorites.

Ears ringing, dust clogging her mouth and throat, Reshmina crawled toward the sound. She found her grandmother lying on the ground, half-covered by the door of an old Soviet truck.

"I figured if I kept singing, someone would find me," her grandmother rasped.

Reshmina pulled the door off her. "Are you all right, Anaa?"

"I may have a broken bone or two," she admitted. "Just let me lie here, Mina-jan."

Reshmina's heart skipped a beat. Her grandmother was as stubborn as a donkey when it came to doctors. She claimed she'd never been sick in her life, but Reshmina knew she just didn't like to make trouble. She might be lying there without a leg right now and not even admit it.

Reshmina patted her grandmother's body just to be sure.

"Stop fussing," Anaa groused.

Reshmina heard whining and crying in the darkness—her brother! Zahir was alive!

"Hush," Reshmina's mother said, her voice heavy. "Anaa, keep singing."

"Mor!" Reshmina cried. She wanted to go to her mother, but where was she?

Reshmina's grandmother sang "Momardene Afghane" again, and Reshmina heard the sound of people crawling to them through the scraps of old Soviet metal that had been scattered by the blast. First came her mother and Zahir. Then Marzia. As Reshmina hugged her family, more people found them: an old couple from next door, a young girl from farther up the steps. Taz too.

For a little while, everyone was too dazed to move or speak. Anaa finished her song, and things grew deathly, oppressively quiet. They couldn't even feel vibrations anymore from the fighting up above.

"Is everyone all right?" Taz asked at last. "What's happened? I still can't see."

"I don't know," Reshmina told him. "We can't see either. It's completely dark. Wait," she remembered. "The flashlight!"

Thank God she had put it in her pocket before the explosion. She put her hand in her pocket, but when she touched the flashlight, a sharp pain shot through her palm and she gasped.

"What is it, Mina-jan?" Mor asked in Pashto.

"What's wrong?" Taz asked in English.

Reshmina pulled the flashlight out with her other hand and clicked it on. Everyone squinted again in the bright light. Even Taz, a little.

"Hey—I can see that!" Taz said. "Not great, but I can see a dull glow! I think my eyes are getting better."

Reshmina shined the light on her hand. There was a deep gash across her right palm. It must have happened when part of the ceiling caved in.

"I have a bad cut. On my hand," Reshmina told her mother, then translated for Taz.

Reshmina's mother started to tear a piece of cloth from her tunic for a bandage.

"Wait. I have some Kerlix," Taz told them.

Reshmina didn't know that word, but it was some kind of bandage Taz carried in his pockets. He told her how to use it, and she pushed the gauze into her cut with a hiss of pain.

"Sorry," he told her. "This stuff is good, but if the cut's deep, you may still end up with a scar. See? I've got one too." He held out his hand to show her. He had a long, dirty scar in almost the same place on his palm. "It still aches every now and then, when it's cold and gloomy outside," he told her. "But most of the time . . ."

Taz paused, as though what he was saying brought back a painful memory for him.

"But most of the time you just forget it's there," he finished.

Some of the others in the cave had injuries too. Reshmina did what she could to help them with the bandages Taz had given her.

"Where are all the other people?" Reshmina's mother asked. "There were a lot more of us before."

Reshmina turned the flashlight toward the front of the cave. Where there had once been a large, open cavern filled with old Soviet equipment, now there was just a pile of rocks.

The whole front half of the ceiling had caved in.

Reshmina explored the rockfall, looking for a way

through. She stopped when she saw the legs of some poor soul sticking out from under a boulder, the rest of the woman's body crushed in the cave-in.

Crushed like all the other people who'd been with them in the cave.

And there was no way through. The fallen rocks covered everything.

I've killed us, Reshmina thought. *Everyone we know and love. Mor was right. I brought death to our village when I brought Taz into our home.* She cried silently. She had chosen what was right over what was easy. She had dared to be someone new, someone better, to carve a path for herself. And look at where it had gotten her: buried with her family in a grave of her own making.

Reshmina quickly swept the light away, so no one else could see the body.

"Is it bad?" Taz asked.

Reshmina felt the anger of a hundred souls well up inside her, and she turned on the American soldier.

"*Is it bad?*" she said. "Yes, it's bad! There was only one entrance to this cave, and now we're trapped! We're trapped, and all those other people who were in here with us are *dead*!"

Reshmina picked up a rock from the ground and hurled it at Taz. He still couldn't see well, but he heard the rock strike the wall behind him and flinched.

Reshmina picked up another stone and threw it at him, hitting him in the arm.

"Hey, what—?" he started to ask.

"We're trapped and they're dead and it's all your fault!" Reshmina yelled at him. It wasn't her fault for dreaming. It was *his* fault for being here.

"But I didn't—"

"You and all the other Americans!" Reshmina told him. She threw another rock that clanged off an old Soviet hubcap. "Why don't you get out of Afghanistan? All you're doing is killing us!"

"We're trying to fix things!" Taz argued.

"Things you broke to begin with!" Reshmina told him.

"We're building wells. Roads. Schools!" Taz said. "Probably the school you go to."

"You killed my sister!" Reshmina cried.

Taz looked horrified. "I what? How? When?"

"Not you. Your country," Reshmina said. She was crying now, big wet tears fed by the horrible things that had happened two years ago, and today. "You bombed my sister! She died. So many of our friends did too."

"I'm sorry," Taz told her. "Really, I am. But we're fighting a war against the Taliban. Sometimes innocent people get hurt. We're trying to *help*."

Reshmina burned inside. Was this anger what

Pasoon felt all the time? The fury that had pushed him to join the Taliban?

"You can help us by leaving," Reshmina told Taz. "My village was never bombed until the Americans came!"

"We have to be here," Taz argued. "Do you know the first thing that will happen if the US leaves Afghanistan? There will be another civil war, and the Taliban will take over again. You're too young to remember, Reshmina, but they did awful things. They are bad, bad people."

"I know all about the Taliban!" Reshmina told him. "I know how awful they are."

"Well, if we leave, you'll be right back where you started before we got here."

"But your drones kill as many of us as them," Reshmina said. She held up her injured hand. "You bandage our wounds and want us to say thank you, but you're the reason we were hurt."

Taz was quiet for a moment. "If we can just beat the Taliban. Get Afghanistan back on its feet. Give you a chance to grow . . ."

Reshmina remembered the cedar cone in the graveyard—and the graves from the previous wars. All those invaders who had swept to victory with their superior weapons, only to be driven out again by Afghan fighters.

"You say you have been here for ten years," Reshmina

said. "Your country has been here nearly twice that long. And *still* you haven't won. You never will. Nobody can rule Afghanistan. Not even Afghans. So I ask you again: Why are you still here?"

Taz looked away without answering.

"Zahir! Come away from there!" Reshmina's mother called.

Reshmina shined the flashlight in her little brother's direction. All she could see was his legs, sticking out from under a rock. For a horrible moment, she thought Zahir had been buried like the lady at the front of the cave. But Zahir just had his head in a hole in the wall—a crack that had opened up during the cave-in. Marzia and their mother were able to drag the curious two-year-old out by his ankles.

Reshmina examined the hole with her flashlight, and she gasped.

"What is it? What's under there?" asked a woman standing nearby.

Reshmina felt a tiny spark of hope rekindle in her chest, and she turned excitedly to the others.

"It might be another way out!"

BRANDON

BANANAS AND PINK GRAPEFRUIT

Brandon followed the sound of Woody Guthrie's "This Land Is Your Land" through the darkness and found Richard trapped under part of a wall.

"Help me get him out of here!" Brandon cried.

Together, Brandon, Pratik, and Gayle were able to lift the layers of drywall high enough for Richard to crawl out. When Richard was free, Brandon dropped to his knees and threw his arms around him.

"Brandon!" Richard cried, hugging him back. "I couldn't hear and couldn't see. I thought I'd been blinded and deafened by the blast, so I just started singing. I couldn't even hear myself, but I hoped somebody else would. And you did. You saved my life, kid."

"Now we're even," Brandon said. He wasn't sure

Richard heard him, but he'd make sure he told him again later.

"We need to find one of the exits up onto the street," Pratik told them.

Brandon didn't want to move, didn't want to let Richard go, but he knew they had to get out of here. And he'd kept the others waiting long enough.

Richard was wobbly and had to lean on Brandon to stand, but he could make it.

"Which way do we go? I still can't see a thing," Gayle said.

"What if we walk right into a hole in the floor, and fall down into a subway tunnel?" Pratik asked.

Something *crunched* in the near distance, like rock shifting, and the ceiling groaned.

"I don't think we have a lot of choice," Brandon said.

"We have to try," said Gayle. She took their hands. "Human chain."

Brandon went first. He was closest to the ground and could feel his way as they went. Pratik was the biggest of them, and he took over helping Richard walk.

Brandon moved very slowly, pushing his waterlogged sneakers forward an inch. Then another inch. Then another. The darkness was total and complete. Pratik was right; the blast might have blown holes in the floor. Would he stumble into a hole and fall to his death? Walk straight into a broken window and slice himself into pieces? Brandon had to fight down his panic. The only way out of here was if they all kept their cool.

Brandon kicked things as he went—broken glass, pieces of drywall, wet clothes, soda cups, shoes, boxes with unknown things in them. He called out warnings about obstacles to the others when he could.

Without his sight, Brandon focused on his other senses. He reached out with his hands, but also listened for clues in the sound of the water at their feet and the creaking of the building. He used his nose too. What was that smell? Something made him think of bananas and pink grapefruit, and he frowned. What in the mall would smell like that? He ran through the shop directory in his head. Was there a smoothie place here? No. There was a Ben & Jerry's and a yogurt place, but those were very different smells.

Suddenly he had it, and he stopped.

"We're going the wrong way!" he told the others.

"How do you know?" Pratik asked.

"Smell that? Bananas and pink grapefruit? We're near the Body Shop! That's the smell of hair and hand stuff!"

"Oh my God, he's right," said Gayle. "I can smell the ginger shampoo!"

Brandon turned the group around, following the map in his head. He moved more confidently now, and in his hurry he ran right into something shin-high. Gayle tried to hang onto him, but the thing was big and hard and hollow, and Brandon fell down face-first on top of it.

"Ow!" Brandon cried. His shins screamed in pain, and his right hand where he was cut stung all over again.

"Brandon! You okay?" Richard called.

"Yes," Brandon grunted.

A fuzzy wet furball bumped into his arm in the water, and Brandon jerked back in disgust. *A rat!* New York City was full of rats. There had to be a bunch of them down here right now, trying to survive like Brandon and the others. The thought horrified him, and he scrambled to get away. In his panic, his hand brushed another of the furballs, and he felt its big fingers.

Its big fingers?

Brandon put his hand back out in the darkness, afraid but curious, and felt for one of the furry things. It had arms and legs and big cloth eyes and teeth, and a tag sewn into the side. Brandon sagged with relief. He would have laughed if he hadn't been so afraid. He'd been frightened by a harmless stuffed animal!

Gayle helped him back to his feet, and Brandon ran his hands over the big, hollow thing he'd run into. It had all kinds of weird curves and contours, and was slick and cool and smooth, like fiberglass covered with a varnish. What was Brandon touching?

A very recent memory came back to him, and he turned excitedly to the others.

"It's the statue of Bugs Bunny!" Brandon said.

"We're at the Warner Bros. Store! We're going in the right direction!"

They couldn't get past the debris near the Sunglass Hut, but Brandon knew there was another way around, past the FILA store with its sportswear and sneakers. That would take them right to the exit to Vesey Street, next to the Duane Reade. They could get out there!

Brandon told the others the plan, and they were off again. Brandon went slowly. Achingly slowly. But he wasn't eager to repeat his Bugs Bunny collision with something that could be a lot more dangerous—like the railing to the PATH escalators.

Deet-deet-deet-doot. De-de-deet-doot.

The sound of a cell phone ringing out in the darkness made them all jump, then stop in their tracks.

"It's a Nokia," said Pratik. "My wife has one just like it. She's not here, thank God," he added.

Deet-deet-deet-doot. De-de-deet-doot.

The phone kept ringing.

"What do we do?" Brandon asked.

"See if you can get to it," Richard told him.

Deet-deet-deet-doot. De-de-deet-doot.

Brandon changed course, veering slightly off to the left. He got closer, closer—and then the ringing stopped. He froze and waited.

"Do we—" he started to ask, and then—

Deet-deet-deet-doot. De-de-deet-doot.

The phone started ringing again. Brandon homed in on it in the darkness, leading the human chain closer and closer, inch by inch, until his foot ran into something big and hard. He put his hands out and felt around, and Gayle and the others did the same.

Deet-deet-deet-doot. De-de-deet-doot.

The phone was buried under a pile of rubble. Along with whoever had been carrying it.

"I think I found a part of the ceiling, but I can't lift it," Pratik said, straining.

"I can't even see what to lift," said Richard.

"We have to leave them for the rescue workers when they get here," Gayle said quietly.

If they get here, Brandon added in his head. From the way no one spoke, he wondered if they were all thinking the same thing.

They came together again in their human chain, and Brandon led them away while the phone continued to ring behind them: *Deet-deet-deet-doot. De-de-deet-doot.* Somebody somewhere outside the towers, desperately dialing a number again and again that would never be answered.

A few minutes later, Brandon found the corner of what he guessed was the FILA store. When he made the turn into the next hallway, he saw a small fire in one of the restaurants down the way. It was the Sbarro! Brandon had taken them the right way!

"We're almost there!" Brandon told his friends.

They inched closer. The fire wasn't big, but it was a beacon in the darkness. *Probably a grease fire*, Brandon thought, like the one he'd seen that morning in Windows on the World. The last time he'd seen his dad. He swallowed the memory. He had to focus on getting out, leading his friends to safety.

A pile of debris blocked the exit up to Vesey Street, but there was enough light from the fire in the Sbarro to pick their way up and over the rubble. When they were on the other side, they could see daylight at the top of the escalator.

"We made it!" Pratik cried.

Brandon wanted to sink to his knees in thanks and exhaustion, but they couldn't stop yet. Not when they were so close.

Still holding hands, they hurried up the stairs toward the sunlight at the top. They came out on Vesey Street, right across from the post office, and laughed and cried and hugged each other.

They were *out*. Out of the mall, out of the Twin Towers, out of danger. They had survived!

But something was wrong—very, very wrong. Soon they all began to notice it and stopped celebrating.

A thick, heavy smoke cloud hung over Lower Manhattan. Outside had looked bright when they were underground, but now that they were up on the street, the sky was so dim it felt like twilight.

It looked too like somebody had driven a tank through the city. Trash cans and cars were crushed, lampposts were bent, bus stops were broken, and trees were shattered. And *everything* was covered with a fine, light gray dust. A fire truck and an ambulance parked in the middle of Vesey Street were coated in the same stuff, their red lights still flashing underneath the thin layer of gray. The dust reminded Brandon of snow. Not just the way it blanketed everything, but how it made things quiet too. Muffled the sounds of the city. Manhattan was never quiet—not even at night. But now it felt as quiet and still as the underground mall had been after the blast.

Something else was wrong too.

"Where are all the people?" Gayle whispered.

There were footprints in the dust, but the streets were empty. There were always people in Manhattan. Millions of them. Now there were none.

Pratik turned and took a step back. "Oh my God," he whispered.

Brandon looked up. It took his brain a long moment to process what he was seeing—or what he *wasn't* seeing. What was *supposed to be* in the big empty slice of the Manhattan skyline but wasn't there anymore.

The South Tower of the World Trade Center was gone. The whole 107-floor skyscraper had collapsed.

RESHMINA

WE'RE HERE BECAUSE WE'RE HERE

Reshmina wriggled through the hole in the cave wall and fell clumsily to the floor of another room. She paused for a long moment, scared to move. She had no idea what was in this hidden chamber, but she had to see if it led to some way out.

Her mother handed the flashlight to her through the hole. "Be careful, Mina-jan!"

"We'll work on widening the entrance from this side, just in case," Taz told her, and Reshmina heard him begin to chip away at the rock.

Reshmina clicked on the flashlight, and a bright white ghost with soulless eyes stared back at her.

Reshmina screamed and dropped the flashlight.

"Mina-jan?" her mother called. "Mina-jan, are you all right?"

"Reshmina?" Taz called.

Reshmina grabbed her chest and waited for her heart to stop trying to thump its way out of her. The flashlight was still on but pointed away from whatever she had seen, and she was afraid to pick it up again. But the thing was still there, right in front of her in the dark.

"Reshmina?" her mother called again.

With shaking hands, Reshmina picked up the flashlight and pointed it up at the ghost.

Reshmina exhaled. It wasn't a ghost at all. It was just a statue. A statue carved out of white marble, with blank, empty eyes.

"I'm all right," Reshmina told her mother. "I just . . . saw something that scared me. I'm all right," she added in English, for Taz.

The shiny white statue was the top half of a bare-chested man wearing a toga. His face was young, his nose was long and flat, and his stone hair was curly.

Reshmina hadn't seen anything like it before. Islamic art almost never included human figures, so this statue must have been very old. From the time when the Greeks had invaded and ruled Afghanistan, perhaps? But that was *thousands* of years ago. Had this statue really been sitting here, hidden away in this cave all that time?

"What's in there?" Taz asked.

"An old statue," Reshmina called back to him. "And other things too."

Reshmina played the flashlight over the artifacts in the room, relics of times long past she knew only from her history lessons. There was a round brass shield with a black winged horse painted on it that must have been from ancient Greece. Next to that was a white pith helmet, like the kind British soldiers had worn when they had invaded Afghanistan two hundred years ago. Along the far wall were a few old English Enfield rifles, and next to that was a stack of curved bows, like the kind the Mongols had once wielded in their conquest of Afghanistan. There were Soviet weapons here too—rusty old land mines and automatic rifles and belts of bullets. Like the statue, everything was covered by a thin gray dust.

Nobody had been in this room in a long, long time.

On the other side of the wall, Taz sang softly.

We're here because we're here because
we're here because we're here.
We're here because
we're here because
we're here because we're here.

"What is that song?" Reshmina asked softly. She didn't know why, but this room made her want to whisper.

"It's nonsense, really," said Taz. "Something I heard

my sergeant singing years ago, when I came back for my third tour of duty. It comes from World War I. The soldiers in the trenches sang it while they were waiting to be sent charging straight into the enemy machine guns. The tune is something we sing on New Year's Eve. 'Auld Lang Syne.' Do you know it?"

"No," Reshmina said.

Taz sang another song.

Should auld acquaintance be forgot,
and never brought to mind?
Should auld acquaintance be forgot,
and auld lang syne.

The lyrics didn't make any sense to Reshmina, but she didn't ask. She searched the chamber for a way out while Taz kept talking.

"The soldiers back in World War I, they changed the words of 'Auld Lang Syne' to 'We're here because we're here because we're here' because they didn't know why they were fighting," he said. "You asked me why the US is still here. I think we're still in Afghanistan because we got in, and we don't know how to get out. If we stay, it's bad, and if we leave, it's bad. There's no right answer. I think it's the same as those boys back in World War I. We're here because we're here, and we don't know how to leave."

Taz was quiet for a moment. Reshmina's flashlight moved across old military medals and flags and pennants. Little statues of the Buddha. A bust of Lenin, the Russian revolutionary leader. Greek and Persian and English coins. Bits of pottery with colorful drawings and a British pocket watch and a furry Russian cap with a red star on it.

"One of the new guys I knew back at Bagram, a rookie soldier named Garcia," Taz said. "He was born *after* we invaded Afghanistan. He stepped on a roadside bomb that hadn't been there the day before, and now he's dead. He died fighting a war that started before he was *born*. You have to be eighteen to join the army. Eighteen! We're still fighting the same war almost twenty years later, and for what? We're never going to change this place."

As Taz's words sank in, Reshmina realized what this room was. This wasn't an arsenal, like the cave where she and Pasoon had found the Taliban cache. This was a kind of shrine. A memorial to all the armies who had invaded Afghanistan and conquered it, just like Taz and the Americans, only to learn that they could never rule it.

Reshmina's flashlight caught some Pashto words painted on the wall, and she took a step back. The paint was very old and the dialect a little strange, but Reshmina could just read the words. It said, *We are content with conflict. We are content with fear. We are content with blood. But we will never be content with a master.*

"Reshmina, do you see any way out?" her mother called.

There was no other entrance to this little room. But there *was* a little crack in the wall at the back. Reshmina clicked off her flashlight, and—yes! She saw a tiny sliver of daylight through the crevice.

"This wall," she called. "It leads outside! If we can just break through it."

"I'll come through," Taz said. "I can chip away at it like I did this one."

THOOM. THOOM. THOOM.

The cave shook with more blasts from above. Apparently the fighting wasn't over. Dirt and rock rained down from the ceiling of the cave, right around the little hole to the other room. The statue of the Greek half-man toppled to the ground with a thud, and the shield clattered as it fell.

"I don't think we have time for that!" Reshmina yelled to Taz.

She spied something in the beam of her light—an old Soviet land mine—and it gave her an idea.

"Stay there!" she told Taz.

Reshmina propped the flashlight on the Greek statue's head and carefully, gently, dragged the land mine over to the crack in the far wall. She wedged the land mine into the crack, then picked up the Greek shield.

The leather straps inside had long since dried out and broken, but Reshmina was still able to hold it up by the metal buckles on its back.

POOM. POOM. More explosions rocked the cave from above.

"Reshmina, what are you doing?" her mother cried from the other side. "The ceiling's falling apart in here!"

"Get as far away from the entrance as you can!" Reshmina called back to her mother. "I'm going to try to blow a hole in the other wall!"

"*You're what?*" Mor cried.

There was a partial wall toward the back of the chamber, and between that and the shield, Reshmina hoped she would be protected enough from the mine. Now she just needed something to activate it. There weren't any big rocks around, but the bust of Lenin would do nicely. Reshmina picked it up and said a silent prayer. Her hand still stung from the gash, but she swallowed the pain, lobbed Lenin's head toward the land mine, and ducked down behind the wall, the shield held tight over her head.

Thunk.

Lenin missed.

Reshmina closed her eyes, her heart thumping in her chest. She'd been ready for an explosion, and then nothing! Still holding the shield, she got up to get Lenin and try again.

THOOM. THOOM. THOOM.

Big explosions outside rocked the cave again, and this time a little piece of the ceiling broke off right above the crack in the wall. The rock fell on the land mine, and—*KABOOM!*—the land mine exploded, and Reshmina went flying.

BRANDON

THE FALLEN TOWER

Brandon stood and stared.

The South Tower was gone. Like some sort of awful magician's trick, it had just disappeared. Disappeared and been replaced by a mountain of concrete and twisted metal, shrouded in a cloud of dust and smoke.

That was what must have knocked them all down in the basement, Brandon realized. What had destroyed the underground mall. The tornado that had hit them was the blast from the South Tower coming down half a block away.

Gayle choked back a sob. "All those people."

Brandon felt all the relief from his escape drain out of him, replaced by an icy chill.

"Maybe people made it out," Richard said. "If they had time?"

Brandon glanced at his watch. Its face was cracked, but the digital readout still worked. It was 10:25 a.m. It had been a little over an hour and a half since the first plane hit. How long after that had the second plane hit? He tried to remember. Fifteen, twenty minutes? The people in the South Tower had had less than an hour to escape before the whole building had come down.

Brandon looked up. The North Tower still poured black smoke into the sky above him. Brandon's father was up there at the top, in Windows on the World. He was still alive. He had to be! The South Tower had fallen—incredibly, unbelievably—but the North Tower was still standing. Brandon had passed those firemen on the stairs. They would get to the fire and get to Brandon's dad. But if the South Tower had fallen . . .

"Oh my God," Pratik said. "Look!"

Pratik pointed toward the middle of the North Tower. Mixed in with the falling metal and glass were things that were moving. *People*, Brandon realized. People were still jumping from the tower, falling ninety floors to their deaths. They dropped out of the thick black smoke that engulfed the top of the building with alarming speed, arms and legs flailing. Brandon saw one man reaching, grabbing as he fell, too far from anything to stop himself, his tie sticking straight up in the air above him.

"I need to find a phone booth," Brandon said,

blinking away the nightmare. He turned to Richard. "I need to call my dad!"

"We need to get out of here first," Richard told him. "Get to my house. We can call your dad from there. My family will be there. You can stay the night with us, and . . . well, we've got some things to work out, but you can stay with me and my family for as long as you need to."

Brandon cried. He cried because Richard was being so nice to him, and because he didn't want to think about what would happen if his dad really did die in the North Tower.

An EMT wearing a white surgical mask hurried up to Gayle and took her by the elbow to sit her down on the curb. Another EMT ran over to Brandon, Richard, and Pratik and handed them little white masks like she and the other EMT wore. The masks were flimsy and thin and wrapped around your ears with an itchy elastic band, but they filtered the awful, gritty air.

"Don't breathe the dust!" the EMT told them. "It's toxic!"

The EMT found the bloody shirt wrapped around Brandon's hand. He stood like a zombie as she peeled it away and treated his wound. Brandon's eyes fell on a banged-up, cylindrical piece of machinery sitting right in the middle of the street. It was as tall as he was, and looked like a crumpled soda can. Brandon struggled to grasp what he was seeing. Was that an *airplane engine* from one of the planes that had hit the Twin Towers? Could one of them have really shot out all this way?

The EMT put something on Brandon's hand that made it sting, and he hissed in pain. She had it wrapped and bandaged in no time though and gave him a quick examination to see if there was anything else that needed patching.

"Can I move this to look at your other hand?" she asked, pulling at something Brandon didn't know he was holding.

Brandon looked down. In his left hand, he carried the little stuffed animal he'd picked up in the wreckage in the underground mall. It was the Tasmanian Devil, a character from the Warner Bros. cartoons. Brandon stared at the wild, silly look on its face. It was like something from another planet, one where airplanes didn't crash into buildings and skyscrapers didn't fall. Why was he still holding it? He'd been so focused on surviving that he hadn't even realized he'd picked it up and taken it with him.

Richard put a hand on Brandon's shoulder. "You should keep that," Richard told him. "It brought us luck."

Luck? thought Brandon. How could anybody think he'd been lucky?

There was a sudden *CRACK* from high above, and

somebody screamed. Brandon looked up. The tall red-and-white antenna on top of the North Tower was just visible, sticking out through the cloud of gray-and-black smoke that billowed from the upper floors. Brandon watched as the giant antenna tilted, leaned, and then disappeared down into the smoke as the top floor of the North Tower fell in on itself.

THOOM. THOOM. THOOM. THOOM.

Brandon felt each boom in his stomach as the top floors of the North Tower collapsed, one by one, under the massive weight of each new falling floor, and then it was a rushing, expanding avalanche. Concrete crumbled to powder in an instant, exploding outward like a blooming flower, and giant pieces of rock and steel came shooting out like fireworks.

The North Tower was coming down.

"No no no no no" was all Brandon could say, all he could think. Then the sound of the individual floors collapsing became a rumble, a tidal wave, a static roar, and Brandon's heart stopped as he watched one hundred and seven stories, along with five hundred thousand tons of concrete and steel and moldy carpets and computers and human beings, come straight down. All around him, the cars on the street shuddered and bounced. The gray cloud from the tower expanded out, out, out, and then the cloud of dust and rock and glass came blasting across the plaza and down the narrow streets between

Manhattan's surviving skyscrapers like a living thing, coming to swallow Brandon.

Like it had swallowed his father.

"Run, Brandon!" Richard cried. *"Run!"*

Brandon ran. He had never been so scared in all his life. Not when he had been trapped in the elevator. Not when he had almost fallen off the edge of the 89th floor. Not when he'd been battered and blind in the underground mall. The thing that had killed his father was coming for him, chasing him like a giant monster through the streets of Manhattan, and he ran in a wild panic down Vesey Street, straight away from the thing that hunted him. Car alarms went off all around him, honking, beeping, flashing, like they were yelling at him to *RUN. RUN. RUN.* Then the sun went out in the sky and darkness surrounded him, and the air turned to ash in his mouth despite his white mask.

I'm going to die, Brandon thought.

He was just to the little old church called St. Paul's, halfway down the long block to Broadway, when the full force of the blast caught up to him. *FWOOMPH.* The wind picked Brandon up and threw him down the street as though he weighed no more than a leaf. Brandon tumbled, skidded, bounced, rolled. Everything was a blur of asphalt and ash and pain, and then he slammed into a honking car and bounced off, sliding to a stop in the middle of the street.

Brandon wrapped his battered arms around his chest and tucked his head down as the monster roared over him, past him. Paper and ash fluttered in its wake, and then it was gone and Brandon lay alone in the street, covered from head to foot in white dust.

Brandon's arms and legs shook as he got up on all fours to look around. Everything was covered in another coat of fine white dust, including the lump of a body that lay in the street a few yards back.

"Richard?" Brandon cried.

Brandon stood, staggered, limped back to the unmoving form, his feet leaving drag marks in the soot and ash. Manhattan was quiet again, silent as a grave. That's what this place was now—a giant grave for the thousands of people who hadn't been able to escape before the towers fell.

Brandon just prayed Richard hadn't joined them.

Brandon fell to his knees next to the body of his friend. Richard lay facedown on the road, motionless. Brandon put a hand to Richard's back and shook him gently.

"Richard?" he whispered. "Richard, please be alive." Brandon couldn't take it if Richard had died too.

Richard's fingers twitched, and his arm slid out across the ash-covered asphalt, looking for something. Brandon didn't know what Richard was looking for, but he was alive. *Richard was alive.*

Brandon put his hand in Richard's, and Richard squeezed it. Richard relaxed then, stopped looking for whatever he'd been looking for, and Brandon took Richard's hand in both of his and wept, the tears carving tracks down the white dust that covered his face. Because Brandon knew then what Richard had been looking for when he'd put his arm out.

He had just wanted to know, like Brandon, that his friend was all right, and that they were together.

RESHMINA

9/11

Reshmina blinked awake in the bright sunshine. She lay on the ground by the river, near the fields with their corn and barley and rice that had yet to be harvested. Her ears rang and her body ached, but she was alive. So was her mother, who was sitting by her side.

Her mother wrapped Reshmina up in a hug so tight it hurt.

"That was a very brave and very foolish thing you did," Mor told her.

Taz stood behind them both, smiling.

"What happened?" Reshmina asked him.

"A big boom," Taz told her. "That wall you hid behind took the worst of it. The mine blew a hole in the outer wall just big enough for us all to climb through. Too tight for me to make it with my battle belt on though." The belt he had worn with all the pouches on it was gone, and he tucked his thumbs into his beltless pants. "Had to leave it behind."

One more artifact for the shrine to failed conquerors, Reshmina thought.

She sat up suddenly. "What about the others? Zahir, Marzia, Anaa—"

"They're all right," Reshmina's mother told her, and Reshmina saw now that there were other American and Afghan soldiers among them, treating the survivors for cuts and bruises. Taz was bandaged up too. Reshmina put a hand to her aching head. How long had she been out?

"Your eyes—" Reshmina said to Taz. He was cleaned up and looking directly at her, and for the first time she saw that his eyes were a brilliant blue.

"Oh, yeah," he said with a smile. "I'm beginning to see the light."

Anaa, Marzia, and Zahir crowded around her. Reshmina's grandmother, sister, and brother squeezed her hands and touched their heads to hers.

"Baba!" Zahir cried, waving at someone behind Reshmina.

Her heart leaped, and she turned. Coming around the bend in the road was her father, along with other men from the village. Baba was alive! Marzia and Zahir ran to hug him, and after Reshmina was able to get to her feet, she and her mother followed.

"Baba! I was so worried about you!" Reshmina cried, giving him a hug.

"And I you, Mina-jan. We couldn't find you, but then we heard the explosion." Baba looked around. "Where is Pasoon?"

Reshmina felt the blood drain away from her face. *Pasoon.* Had he been with the Taliban during the gunfight? Was his body lying on a hillside somewhere, filled with American bullets?

"Pasoon went to the Taliban," she told her father.

Baba sagged against his crutch. "Yes. I worried he might."

"I tried to stop him, Baba. I followed him. Tried to talk him out of it." Reshmina fought back her tears. "Nothing I said would change his mind."

Baba put a hand on her head. "I know, Mina-jan. I know."

"I wanted to do the right thing," Reshmina said, "but all I did was lead everyone to their deaths! Everyone in the village is dead because of me!"

"No, no, Mina-jan," Baba said. "Come and see."

He took her by the hand and led her around the bend, where dozens of villagers had come out of the front entrance to the cave. The cave-in had only separated Reshmina and the others from the rest of the villagers, not killed everyone on the other side!

"A few died, yes," Baba told her. "To God we belong,

and to God we return. But many more survived, and thanks to you."

Reshmina buried her face in her father's tunic to hide her tears.

"We are safe now," Baba said. "The Americans are clearing the village of the last of the Taliban."

Reshmina turned around. Taz had been standing off to the side, and now three more American soldiers came over to join him. One of them playfully swatted the little brown stuffed animal strapped to Taz's vest. The white strip on the soldier's vest said his name was CARTER. He wore his body armor over a jacket with the sleeves cut off, and Reshmina saw the word INFIDEL tattooed on one of his muscular arms. *Infidel* was what the mujahideen called anyone who didn't follow Islam.

Carter shook his head. "What a mess, huh, Taz?"

"I know," said Taz. "And today of all days."

"Oh," Carter said. "Right. Jeez."

Reshmina remembered Taz saying that exact same thing when she'd first brought him home. "What do you mean?" she asked him. "'Today of all days'?"

"Today's 9/11," Taz said, like that meant something.

"I don't understand," Reshmina told him.

"*Nine-eleven*," Taz said. "Nine for the month, eleven for the day. September 11th. Today's the anniversary of the attack on the World Trade Center."

Reshmina shook her head. "I don't know what that is."

"Are you serious?" Taz asked. "The Twin Towers? The airplanes?"

Reshmina still had no idea what he was talking about.

Taz frowned, and he and Carter shared a confused look.

"How could you not know about 9/11?" Carter asked Reshmina. He was almost angry about it.

"9/11 is . . . it's the whole reason I'm here," Taz told Reshmina. "The whole reason any of us are here." He ripped open another Velcro pouch on his vest and pulled out two pieces of paper. One was a thin, glossy page from a magazine. It showed a photograph of two gray, rectangular buildings, each twice as tall as the other buildings around them. Black smoke poured from both, blowing sideways in the wind.

Behind the buildings was bright blue cloudless sky, like today.

Taz showed her the picture like it should mean something to her, but it didn't. She'd never seen these buildings in her entire life.

"She's a kid," said Carter. "She just hasn't learned about it in school yet," he told Taz.

But when Taz showed the picture to Mor and Baba, they'd never heard of 9/11 either. Neither had Anaa, nor an elderly couple who'd been with them in the cave. Baba called the other villagers over, but none of them knew what 9/11 was, or why the Americans were so angry about it.

"That's the World Trade Center in New York City," Taz told them, tapping the photo. He was scowling now. He looked a little like Pasoon when he was angry, Reshmina thought. "Terrorists flew two planes into the Twin Towers, one into each building. Three thousand people died in the attacks. *My dad* died in the attacks."

"Your father?" Reshmina said.

Taz showed Reshmina the other photo he carried, this one of a man and a boy in nice clothes. A father and son. The father had a broad chest, brown skin, and a nice smile—just like Taz. The little boy in the picture had high cheekbones, brown hair, and blue eyes. Also like Taz.

"I was there that day," Taz said. "In the North Tower. I made it out, but my dad didn't."

Beside him Carter looked at Taz with a kind of reverence. Almost awe.

Taz traced his fingers over the man in the photo. "That's him. My dad: Leo Chavez. He worked in a restaurant all the way at the top of the North Tower."

"Chavez?" Reshmina repeated. "Your name is Lowery."

Taz nodded. "That's my adopted name. I took it in honor of the guy who helped me get out of the towers. He adopted me a year later. Richard Lowery. My name's Brandon Lowery now."

"We just call him Taz," said Carter.

Reshmina looked again at the photos. If someone had done this to her village, to her baba, she would feel the same anger, the same sadness. She explained the pictures to her family and the other villagers in Pashto, and they nodded with understanding.

"So it is badal, then. That is why they are here," Anaa said.

Reshmina sighed. The Americans didn't follow Pashtunwali, but apparently revenge was something they knew and practiced as well. And who could blame them?

"Afghans did this to you?" Reshmina said sadly. "The Taliban?"

Taz shifted and looked uncomfortable. "Well, no," he admitted. "It wasn't the Taliban. The men who flew the planes into the buildings, they were mostly from Saudi Arabia. A group called al Qaeda. But the Taliban hated America and the West as much as al Qaeda did," Taz explained. "The Taliban let al Qaeda set up their terrorist headquarters here. The al Qaeda leader, Osama bin Laden, he planned the September 11 attacks right here in Afghanistan." Taz glanced around. "The Taliban government wouldn't hand bin Laden over to the US, so we invaded."

Reshmina's anger flared like a brush fire. "Wait," she said. "This Osama bin Laden and al Qaeda, they destroyed these buildings, killed three thousand people. That is terrible. *Unforgivable.* The curse of God and all his angels and of the whole people upon them." She spat on the ground. "But how many more of our buildings have you destroyed in return? How many more Afghan people have you killed?"

Taz was quiet. Beside her, Reshmina's family looked on with concern. She knew they didn't comprehend her words, but they could hear the anger and confrontation in them.

"You said yourself," Reshmina continued. "Afghans did not do this attack. You are seeking revenge against the wrong people! Did you find and kill this man? This Osama bin Laden?"

"Yes," Taz said quietly.

"When?"

"Almost ten years ago. In Pakistan."

"Then why are you here?" Reshmina asked again.

"Hey, if you're not with us, you're against us," Carter said.

Taz looked away, and Reshmina waited. Did Taz agree with his friend? Or was his answer still "We're here because we're here"? What kind of excuse was that when people on both sides were dying? When Hila was dead?

"So if the United States does to my country what this Osama bin Laden and his al Qaeda did to yours,"

Reshmina asked, "does that mean Afghanistan now gets to invade your country in retaliation for your attack?"

Carter laughed. "What? No."

"Of course not," Reshmina said bitterly. "Because the rules are different for the United States. You make your own rules."

"Damn right we do," said Carter.

Reshmina looked at Taz, but he couldn't meet her eyes. It wasn't right, and he knew it.

The walkie-talkie on Carter's body armor squawked to life. "Carter, this is Pacheco," the voice on the other end said. "We've got a house at the top of the village with at least five insurgents holed up inside it. No civilians in range. Over."

Carter held a button on his walkie-talkie and stepped away to respond, but Reshmina could hear what he said. "Acknowledged. Pull back and I'll call in a bird. Over." Carter waited a moment, then spoke into his walkie-talkie again. "Base, this is Carter. We need a strike on a building with at least five insurgents in it. Pacheco will call in coordinates. Over."

In moments, Reshmina heard the familiar thrum of an incoming Apache.

WHOMP-WHOMP-WHOMP-WHOMP. The helicopter thundered up along the river and hovered right over their heads. Everyone ducked and backed away from the downdraft, and a second later came the hiss and whoosh of a single missile streaking out from under the metal grasshopper's wings. The missile struck a house at the top of the village, and it exploded in a burst of fire and rock.

Reshmina let out a breath. It was over now, right?

Suddenly, there was a loud CRACK, and Reshmina watched in horror as the house beneath the shattered building crumbled and fell. The house underneath that collapsed under the weight of the first two, and the demolished buildings took out the next house, and the next, and the next, until the whole village became one great avalanche, falling down on itself.

Carter cursed and turned to everyone standing around watching. "Run! Get across the river!" he cried.

The villagers ran from the landslide, into the fields. Taz ran with Reshmina and her family. When they were safe, they all turned and watched as the village slid down into nothing, swallowed by a great brown cloud of dust that came roaring at them like a lion.

The helicopter hovered a moment more, then lifted away. Its blades churned the smoke and dust as it left, and through a brief gap in the cloud Reshmina saw the empty hillside where her village had once been.

Everything she had ever known was gone.

"Dadgum," Carter said. "Bombed 'em back up to the Stone Age." He clapped Taz on the shoulder. "That's for 9/11," Carter added.

Carter and the other American soldiers headed back across the river while Taz waited behind.

"Reshmina, I'm sorry," Taz said. He looked horrified. "That was *not* supposed to happen."

"And yet it did," Reshmina said.

"I'm sorry," Taz said again, and he left to join his people.

Reshmina's legs gave out, and she sank to her knees. Around her, the other villagers cried out and sobbed.

If the Americans had named their helicopters "Apaches" for some tribe they had defeated in battle, Reshmina thought, they should call their next helicopters "Afghans." Because the United States had surely destroyed Afghanistan.

BRANDON

FOR, NOT AGAINST

Brandon and Richard walked hand in hand down empty Manhattan streets. They were both dazed, and neither of them had spoken for blocks. Soon they came to a small city park with lush green trees and red and yellow flowers. Richard found someone who let him borrow a cell phone, and he stepped aside to try to reach his family again.

Brandon stood like a statue, staring at the flowers. The park was beautiful, but it brought him no pleasure to see it or to be there.

"Talisha!" Richard cried into the phone. He had finally gotten through to his wife. "Oh my God, honey, I never thought I'd hear your voice again . . . Yes—yes. I'm all right. I'm safe."

But are *we all right?* Brandon wondered. *Are we*

really safe? He looked around at that park, just blocks away from the burning pit where thousands of people had just died—where his *father* had just died—and wondered how anybody could ever feel happy and safe again. This little oasis wasn't the real world. Brandon knew that now. He had seen the real world. It was dark and evil and scary, not sunshine and flowers waving in the breeze.

"Yes," Richard was saying into the phone. "I'm with a boy who escaped with me. Brandon. I'm bringing him home. It'll be a while—the subways and buses aren't running . . . No, don't leave the house. We'll walk it . . . All right . . . Yes—I love you too."

Brandon and Richard got moving again. They decided to get out of Manhattan as quickly as possible, following the thousands of other people streaming out of the city over the Brooklyn Bridge. They didn't use the pedestrian path. They walked right down the middle of the road instead, working their way around abandoned cars. Some of the people walking by them cried. Others talked in whispers. Most just held their shirts to their faces and walked away from Manhattan as fast as they could, bewildered and stunned.

It felt like the end of the world.

Brandon was still holding Richard's hand as they walked into the little front yard of his house in Queens three hours later. The security door flew open and Richard's wife, Talisha, came running down the steps.

She was a pretty Black woman with curly hair, wearing jeans and a purple sweater. Brandon recognized her from the photo on Richard's desk. A small white dog ran out onto the porch next, followed by Richard's little daughter and son. The kids waited awkwardly, not really sure why their father coming home today was a bigger deal than usual.

"Thank God you're alive!" Talisha said, and wrapped Richard in a hug. Brandon looked away as they kissed.

Richard's wife pulled away at last, her eyes full of tears.

"Brandon, this is my wife, Talisha," Richard said. "Brandon saved my life," he told his wife.

"Then I thank God for you too," Talisha said, giving Brandon a hug and kissing the top of his head. He closed his eyes and scrunched a little lower, embarrassed, but he didn't fight it.

"He saved my life first," Brandon said.

"You can tell me all about it after we get you both cleaned up," Talisha said. She took Brandon's and Richard's hands and pulled them toward the porch. Richard embraced his children and introduced them to Brandon as Kiara and Anthony. Richard also petted the happy little dog, whose name was Neo.

Richard's house was small but cozy. Brandon caught flashes of it as he was led inside—shelves full of books, dolls and toy cars on the floor, family pictures on the walls—but it was all a blur. He was exhausted, and he was losing his focus on the world.

Richard's daughter and son followed on Brandon's heels. Neo jumped to sniff at the Tasmanian Devil Brandon still carried.

"Are you a ghost?" Kiara asked.

"Hush now," Talisha told her. "Let him be." She steered Brandon into a bathroom with an old claw-foot tub and a shower curtain on a metal ring. "Get yourself cleaned up, and then we'll get some food in you," Talisha told him.

Anthony and Kiara stared at him, wide-eyed, until the bathroom door shut in their faces, and suddenly Brandon was alone.

He stood for long minutes in the middle of the black-and-white-tiled bathroom, letting the stillness settle over him. For the first time in hours, Brandon wasn't trying to get somewhere or survive. He had gotten used to planes hitting buildings and smoke in the air and people falling from the sky, and now that it was all done he didn't know what to do with himself.

The silence in the bathroom grew. *I should be doing something*, Brandon thought. He just didn't know what. He wasn't hungry, he wasn't sleepy, and he didn't feel like showering. He didn't feel like doing anything but crawling into a ball and disappearing, but he couldn't do that.

So he did nothing.

Brandon caught sight of himself in the mirror and recoiled. Richard's daughter was right—he *did* look like a ghost, covered all over in fine white dust. But it was more than that. There was a hollow, empty look in his eyes, like he was dead inside.

Was his father dead too? Brandon had seen the building come down. But had his father gotten out somehow before it happened? It seemed impossible, but Brandon didn't know for sure. Should he be at home right now, waiting there in case his dad came back?

A gentle knock on the door made Brandon jump.

"You okay in there?" Talisha asked softly through the door.

"Yes," Brandon lied.

He set the Tasmanian Devil on top of the toilet. He turned on the sink faucet and put his hand under the water, watching the blood and dust and grime of the World Trade Center start to wash off him. The hand of a ghost turning back into the hand of a living, breathing boy.

When he was done in the shower, Brandon put on a fresh set of Richard's clothes. Talisha had rolled up the sleeves and cuffs for him, but they were still comically baggy on him. He looked less like a ghost now, but he still felt empty inside, and he didn't know if or how he would ever feel whole again. He had been younger when his mother had died, so young that he hadn't understood why she wasn't coming back. Brandon was old enough now to understand that his father was probably gone from his life forever. But unlike the last few months with his mother, Brandon had barely had time to say goodbye to his dad. It was still a fresh wound, deeper and far more painful than the cut on his palm.

"Kid, you done in there?" Richard asked through the door.

Brandon hated to leave the sanctuary of the bathroom, but he couldn't stay in there forever. He opened the door.

Richard had cleaned up too and was wearing jeans and a T-shirt. Richard reached a hand out to Brandon, and they hugged again. Neither of them had to ask, or say why.

"Esther's okay," Richard said at last. "I just talked to her. She and Anson and Mr. Khoury made it out and away from the building before it came down. Anson's dog too."

Brandon nodded. He'd forgotten all about them with all the other things that had happened, and a relief he hadn't expected flooded through him. *That's three people, at least.*

"I need to call my apartment," Brandon said. His voice was thin and raspy, and he cleared his throat. "I need to leave a message for my dad. In case."

Richard looked like he might say something, then

just nodded. He led Brandon to the phone in the kitchen and left him alone. Brandon dialed his number and waited through the rings, hoping against hope his dad would somehow pick up the phone before the answering machine kicked in.

The call connected, and Brandon held his breath.

"Hey, this is Leo Chavez," his dad said.

"And this is Brandon Chavez!" Brandon's recorded voice said.

"Leave us a message!" they said together.

Brandon sniffed. He knew his father wouldn't be there, but he had wanted so badly for him to answer.

"Hey, Dad, it's me. Brandon," he said. Tears came to his eyes, and he blinked them away. "I got out, just like you told me to. I'm okay. I'm with Richard, the guy you talked to. His family's nice. I'm at their house. If you get this, you can call me back at this number," he said, knowing the machine would list it.

Brandon paused. He didn't know what else to say, and the machine was going to cut him off soon. *He's not going to hear this anyway*, Brandon thought, choking back more tears.

"I love you, Dad," he said at last. "Goodbye."

Brandon hung up and went back to the bathroom and closed the door. He sat on the closed toilet seat until his tears ran dry. Then he cleaned up his face and joined Richard's family in the living room.

Richard and Talisha sat on the couch watching the news on TV, while Kiara and Anthony played with LEGOs on the floor. Brandon sat on the couch too, and Neo jumped into Brandon's lap, tail wagging. Any other day, Brandon would have been delighted to play with a dog, but now it was enough to just put his hand on Neo's warm body and feel his heart beat.

They sat in front of the television for hours, watching and listening and trying to make sense of what was happening. Every channel was talking about the attacks. Even MTV and ESPN switched to nonstop news coverage. From talking head after talking head, Brandon learned everything the world knew so far. Terrorists had hijacked two planes and flown them into the North and South Towers of the World Trade Center. He knew that part. He had been there. *Ground Zero.* That's what they were calling the pile of rubble and twisted steel that remained. They couldn't call it the World Trade Center or Twin Towers anymore. The World Trade Center was gone.

A third plane had crashed into the Pentagon, just like the security guard with the bullhorn had told them. The Pentagon was the headquarters of the US Department of Defense, right outside Washington, DC. The TV showed a picture of the smoking hole in the building. One hundred and twenty-five people were dead.

They still had no idea who, or how many, had died when the Twin Towers came down.

A fourth plane had also been hijacked. When the passengers on that flight used phones on the plane to call their families and tell them terrorists had taken over, they learned about the attacks on the Twin Towers and the Pentagon, and they knew they were next. They told their loved ones they were going to try to take the plane back from the hijackers. A few minutes later—right around the time the South Tower had collapsed, while Brandon and Richard had been in the underground mall—that last plane had crashed into a field in Pennsylvania, killing everyone on board.

The people on the news guessed that the terrorists had chosen those four planes specifically because they were all headed for California from the East Coast, and carried as much explosive jet fuel on board as possible.

It was too much to take in at one time. Too much horror, too much death. And none of it made any sense.

"Who would do this to us?" Brandon asked Richard. On the news, they were guessing it was a group of Islamic extremists called al Qaeda, but no one knew for sure yet. "Why do they hate us?" Brandon asked.

Richard shook his head. "I don't know, kid. I don't know."

Kiara and Anthony had long since grown bored with their toys, and they ran through the room laughing and squealing and chasing each other. Brandon scowled at them. How could they be playing around at a time like this? Why weren't Richard and Talisha telling them to be quiet? To have some respect?

Richard read the anger in Brandon's face and put a hand on Brandon's knee. "They don't understand," he said quietly. "They can't yet. They're too young. They know something bad happened, but they don't get how big this is. You wouldn't either. Not really. Except you were there. Your friends and classmates, they're not going to understand either. Not until they're older. When you go back to school, they're going to be laughing and playing and living their lives like this never happened because they're not old enough to get it. But you do, because you were there. That makes you different. You're going to have to remember that."

Brandon nodded and tried to let go of some of his irritation, but it was hard.

President Bush came on the television later, talking about how America had been attacked because they were a beacon of freedom and opportunity. About how they were going to hunt down the people who did this and bring them to justice.

"This is going to be bad," Richard said. "People are hurt. Angry. And they should be. They want revenge, and so do I. But revenge against *who*?"

Brandon didn't know, but he hated whoever had

done this. He wanted them to pay for everything he'd just been through. He wanted them to pay for what they had done to his dad.

On TV, the president was saying that the country was strong. That anybody who wasn't with the United States was against them. He sounded like Brandon's dad.

We're a team, Brandon. Just you and me. It's us against the world.

Brandon's father was gone now, and so was their team. Brandon was all alone against the world.

But was he? Brandon thought back to everyone who'd been trapped in the elevator with him. The people from Richard's floor. Gayle and Pratik in the mall. All the firefighters, the police, the security guard with the bullhorn, all those paramedics and EMTs—Brandon didn't know if any of *them* had survived, but they had helped *others* survive.

And Richard, of course. He and Brandon had helped each other survive, time and again. And now Richard and his wife had taken Brandon in when he had nowhere else to go.

It isn't me against *the world*, Brandon realized. *It's everyone, working together.* And not *against* the world either, but *for* each other.

That was how they survived.

RESHMINA

GROUND ZERO

Reshmina picked up another rock and tossed it off the pile that used to be her home. The sun had almost set on September 11, 2019, and she and Baba were still digging through the rubble, trying to find anything of value. Anything that could help them survive.

The digging was slow and hard, and all Reshmina had to show for her labor so far was one torn sleeping mat and one crushed metal pot. The work was even harder for her father, but he rolled rocks off the pile with determined patience.

The rest of her family was down in the valley, Mor and Marzia making camp while Anaa watched Zahir. They were going to have to spend at least one night without a roof over their heads. Probably many more.

The American soldiers had stayed, calling in Afghan

National Army forces to help them secure the area. Now a team of Americans was meeting with each of the families who had lost their homes and their possessions, arranging for financial compensation for their losses.

Taz had left to receive proper medical treatment for his wounds, but he was back now. Reshmina could see him climbing the hill toward where she and her father worked. Taz was clean and bandaged and had put on a new uniform, and he carried something over his shoulder.

Reshmina kept her head down and kept moving rocks until Taz was standing right next to her.

"Can I help?" Taz asked.

Reshmina didn't look at him.

"I brought blankets," Taz added. He held out a large duffel bag. "Food. A portable stove."

"Thank you," Reshmina said at last.

Baba nodded to him, and Taz set the bag down and started to help them clear the debris. He had a new rifle on a strap across his back, and when he bent over to move a rock, the rifle slid down in his way.

"I hear some of the villagers are packing up and leaving for Pakistan," Taz said.

It was true. Half the village had already collected their payments from the US Army and set off before dark.

Taz pushed his rifle out of the way again and hefted

a rock. "Are you and your family going to go with them?"

"No," Reshmina told him. "My family has decided to stay here. To rebuild."

"You sound like you don't want to do that."

"Why should we?" Reshmina asked. "Our home will just be destroyed again. If not by you, then by the next country that invades. But there is no future for me in Pakistan either." Reshmina sat back to take a break and catch her breath. "Did you rebuild your fallen towers?"

"The World Trade Center?" Taz asked. "Yes and no. They built one new giant skyscraper at Ground Zero instead."

"Ground Zero?" Reshmina asked. She knew what those words meant, but not together.

Taz stood and pushed his rifle around to his back again. "Ground Zero is like . . . the place where a big bomb goes off, or a big disaster happens. It's what they called the place the World Trade Center used to be, until they built the new tower on top of it."

Ground Zero, Reshmina thought. That was as good a name as any for the pile of rocks she was sitting on. It certainly wasn't a village anymore.

"We can help you," Taz said. "Rebuild your village, I mean. We have machines and stuff for this. I don't know how we'd get them in here . . ."

"Bombed them back up to the Stone Age," Reshmina said. She went back to work, moving rocks. "That's

what one of your people said. Right after your Apache destroyed my village."

"He shouldn't have said that," Taz said quietly. "And it was an accident. We're paying for everything that was lost."

"Yes, I know," Reshmina said. She gestured at the rock pile. "Lost your house and everything in it? Here's 4,724 American dollars. Lose a goat? Our sincere apologies, and here is 106 dollars. Lose a daughter? Here's 1,143 dollars. Not as much as for a son, of course, because girls are not worth as much in Afghanistan."

Taz grimaced at how callous it all sounded, but Reshmina wasn't wrong, and they both knew it. "They'll reward you for saving my life," Taz said. "You and your family. You'll get more money than anyone else."

Reshmina sighed. "What will we do with money?" she asked. "We cannot eat it. We cannot milk it. We cannot ride upon it, or sleep inside it. There is no place to spend it, and nothing to spend it *on*." Taz opened his mouth as if to say something, but Reshmina went on. "Use the money to bribe our way across the border into Pakistan? For what? To live the rest of our lives in a refugee camp? That's if we're lucky and the Taliban doesn't steal the money from us first."

Reshmina picked up a rock and threw it away. "You Americans think you can fix everything by throwing money at it," she added. "But your friend was right.

This *is* like the Stone Age. Because no one will let us get *past* the Stone Age. Not when there is nothing but war. Do you understand? The best thing you can do to help us is leave us alone."

"But the Taliban—" Taz said.

"Will take over when you go. I know," Reshmina said. "But your country helped create the Taliban. You gave them weapons and trained them to drive out the Soviets. We have the old textbooks to prove it. Even when you try to help us, you hurt us. And yourselves. Maybe what we need is for you to stop 'helping' us."

Taz shook his head. "I learned a long time ago that it's not 'us against the world,' Reshmina. It's all of us, together. *For* each other."

Reshmina smiled at Taz. How could he not see it? "You can't help us by rebuilding villages and destroying them at the same time. Look at you," she said. "You can't even help me with both hands right now because your gun keeps getting in the way."

She'd caught Taz pushing his rifle up onto his back again with one hand while he tried to pick up a rock with the other. He froze, realizing what he was doing, and his face went red. Carefully, deliberately, he took off his rifle and set it to one side, then picked up the rock with both hands and chucked it away. He held out his arms, palms up, as if to say, *Look, see? I can help with both hands.*

Reshmina smiled ruefully. "You may be able to do that," she told him, "but your country never will. They help with one hand and hold a gun in the other."

It was Taz's turn to sit down and rest. He studied his dirty hands as he rubbed the rock dust from them.

"When the towers came down, everybody pulled together," he said, as if deep in memory. "Not just Americans, but people all over the world. There was this feeling of unity. America invaded Afghanistan with a *coalition* of countries. But then we turned around and invaded Iraq when we still hadn't captured bin Laden or stopped al Qaeda. By 2010, we *still* hadn't caught the people who planned the World Trade Center attacks. That's when I joined the army. I was eighteen, and I wanted *revenge*."

Reshmina nodded. She understood revenge.

"We got bin Laden a year after that, but the mission wasn't over," Taz went on. "Now it was just this 'War on Terror.' I thought I was fighting the good fight. Making sure what happened to me and my dad all those years ago never happened to anybody else. But now I'm not so sure what I'm doing. Who are we fighting? How do we know we've won?"

Taz picked up a small rock and threw it.

"You know," he said, "on 9/11, after everything happened, I remember wondering, *Why does somebody hate us that bad?* We're the good guys, you know?"

Reshmina put down the rock she was picking up and looked at him through narrowed eyes. *The good guys?*

Taz put his hands up in surrender. "I know, I know. But that's what I mean. After 9/11, everybody said al Qaeda attacked us because they hated our way of life, our freedom. But I've been over here ten years, and I've never heard one single person, Taliban or otherwise, talking about how much they hate America's freedom, or Starbucks coffee, or free elections. You and your family didn't even recognize a picture of New York." Taz shook his head. "In America, we think everybody in the world cares about everything we say and do. But the only thing people here care about is what we say and do *over here*." He looked out at what was left of her village. "My dad once told me a bully is somebody who does whatever they want and never gets in trouble for it. Maybe that's what we are. Maybe we're the bullies."

Reshmina watched Taz for a long moment. "Your country may be," she said at last. "But you are not."

"Thanks," said Taz. "Maybe it's time for me to think about leaving the army." He smiled. "I want to be able to help with both hands."

Another soldier called up the hill. It was almost dark, and the Americans were heading back to their base.

Taz stood. "Listen, the army's got this interpreter program. If you work for the US Army here in

Afghanistan as a translator, you get special permission to come to America when you're done. Go to an American university. Maybe become a US citizen. I don't know all the details, but I could find out. Recommend you for the program when you're old enough. Your English is great. You'd be a natural at it, like the lady you met this morning."

"The lady who is dead," said Reshmina.

"Yeah," said Taz. He lowered his head, no doubt thinking about Mariam and everyone else who had died that morning.

"It's not easy," Taz told her. "But then, nothing really worth it ever is."

Reshmina nodded. Just the thought of going to the United States to study at one of their schools gave her goose bumps. But to do it, Reshmina would have to ally herself with the people who had killed her sister. Destroyed her village.

"Thank you, but no," Reshmina said. She would keep going to school, keep learning English. Perhaps move to Kabul when she was old enough. Maybe even find a way to go to the US or Canada or Australia to study. But it would be on her own terms.

"Well, if you change your mind, let me know," Taz said. "No matter what, I'll come back and help. I promise."

"Thank you for the warning," Reshmina told him.

Taz smiled at her joke. "I deserve that," he admitted.

He unhooked the strange stuffed devil from his vest and gave it to Reshmina.

"Here," Taz said. "This brought me luck once. Of a kind. Maybe it'll bring luck to you too."

Reshmina took the dusty, ratty thing. It wasn't much to look at, and it wouldn't serve her any real purpose, but she knew how important it was to Taz.

"Thank you," Reshmina said. She bowed her head to Taz, then remembered how she'd been taught to say goodbye from her English lessons.

"I will friend you on Facebook," she told him.

Taz laughed and said his thanks and goodbyes to Reshmina's father.

When Taz was gone, Reshmina helped her father stand up. They'd done enough work for now, and it was time to join the rest of their family in the valley.

They started walking, but Baba was slow. The steps had always been hard for him, and now even those were gone—buried under a village's worth of wood and stone.

"Is there any other way down?" Baba asked.

Reshmina scanned the hillside. The sun had almost set. On a ridge across the valley, silhouetted against the orange-yellow sky, Reshmina spotted the lone figure of a boy. He was so far away she could never see his face, but Reshmina knew instantly who it was: Pasoon. She would know her brother anywhere.

So he wasn't dead! And he had come back to check on them. Why? To make sure they were all right? Or to gloat over firing another shot at the American hornet's nest?

Despite everything that had happened, everything Pasoon had done, Reshmina's heart still ached at the sight of him. He was her twin, after all. A piece of her would always be missing when they were apart. But apart they would always be, as long as Pasoon chose revenge.

Pasoon raised a hand to wave to her, but Reshmina turned away.

"Come, Baba," Reshmina told her father. "I've found another path."

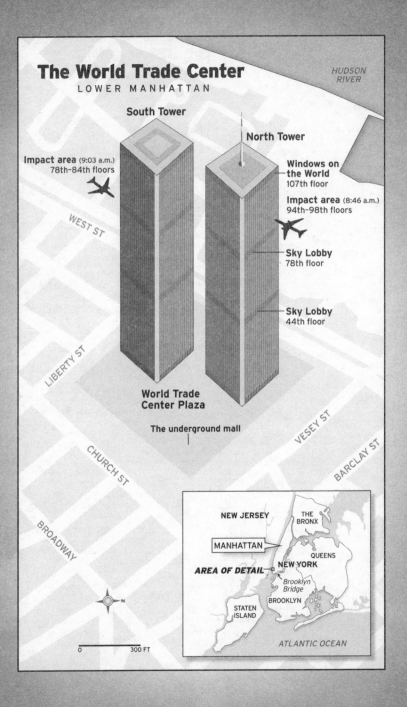

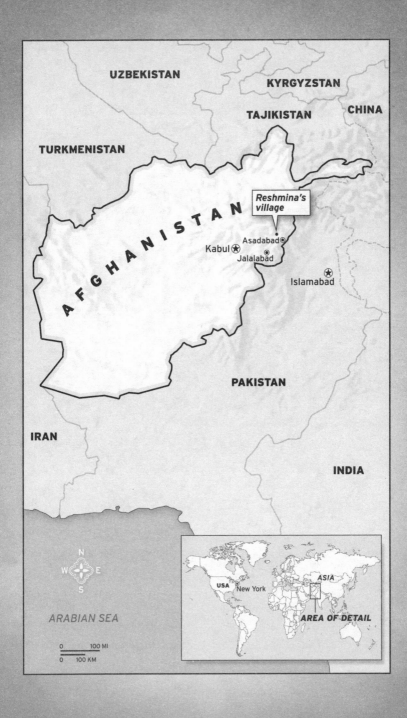

AUTHOR'S NOTE

On September 11, 2001, I was an eighth-grade English teacher in Tennessee. When news of the attacks in New York City hit our school community, we collected the students in the gym, wheeling in blurry TVs with bad reception as all of us—teachers and students—struggled to understand what was happening. No one had a smartphone. There was no Facebook, no Twitter. Instead we turned to one another with the questions we were asking: What was going on? Why would someone do this? Would there be more attacks? Were we now at war? And with whom? What would happen next?

There was only one thing we knew for certain: Nothing would ever be the same.

I tried to write about 9/11 in the years right after 2001, but it always felt too soon. Nearly twenty years later, when my editor and I were discussing what my next novel would be, I finally felt like I was emotionally ready to tell the story of that day—and how the world is different now because of it.

Brandon and Reshmina, along with all the people in their respective stories, are fictional characters. But everything they see and do is based on actual events.

Reshmina's village is fictional but is located in the real Kunar Province, a mountainous part of Afghanistan where the US and its allies have fought a bitter war with the Taliban since 2001. For the sake of story, I have combined a few events from different years in the War in Afghanistan into a single day. The US forward operating base that Pasoon targets with his rifle, for example, would have already been abandoned a few years before he was hired to shoot at it.

Similarly, in Brandon's story, I took the liberty of incorporating a few incidents that took place in the South Tower into the North Tower.

A note on language: Pashto, the language of more than forty million people throughout the world, uses an alphabet based on Arabic script, and there are many different spelling options when transliterating Pashto words into written English. When choosing how to spell a Pashto word in the text, I used the spelling I found most commonly online and in my research.

THE WORLD TRADE CENTER

Made up of seven buildings, the World Trade Center complex opened in 1973 in Lower Manhattan. Its two tallest structures, the 1,368-foot-tall 1 World Trade Center and the 1,362-foot-tall 2 World Trade

Center—known as the North and South Towers—immediately became the tallest buildings in the world. By the time of the attacks in 2001, the complex was home to more than 430 businesses. An estimated 50,000 people worked there, with another 140,000 people passing through as visitors each day—more than the populations of 29 state capitals. The World Trade Center was so big it had its own zip code!

Windows on the World, the restaurant on the top two floors of the North Tower, was a popular dining destination. I went to Windows on the World in February 2001, just seven months before the attacks, when my wife and I were visiting New York City. The views were indeed spectacular. The kitchens in Windows on the World were, in reality, on the 106th floor. I took the liberty of putting them on the 107th floor in Brandon's story.

THE ATTACKS

The World Trade Center symbolized the height of American business and achievement. Perhaps that's what made it such an appealing target for terrorist attacks. In 1993, terrorists detonated 1,500 pounds of explosives in the parking garage underneath the North Tower, with the intention of bringing down both towers. The buildings survived, but the blast destroyed five underground levels of the North Tower, killing six people and injuring more than a thousand.

On the morning of September 11, 2001, terrorists again tried to bring down the towers, and this time they succeeded. Nineteen terrorists armed with box cutters hijacked four passenger planes and deliberately flew two of the planes into the World Trade Center.

The first of the planes, American Airlines Flight 11, slammed into the 96th floor of the North Tower at 8:46 a.m., traveling close to 450 miles per hour and carrying 10,000 gallons of jet fuel, which ignited on impact. The crash instantly killed the 92 people on board the plane and every person on floors 94 to 99 of the tower. Many people on floors right above and below the crash survived but found themselves trapped. None of the 1,402 people on floors 92 through 107 would survive.

Like Brandon, thousands more people below the impact zone were stunned and shaken but alive. No one yet understood just how dangerous the situation was. Emergency operators answering 911 calls that day gave people the same instructions they would give in a regular emergency: Stay where you are and wait for the fire department. In the South Tower, employees who had begun to evacuate when they saw and heard the explosion in the North Tower were told that everything was all right and that they could return to their offices.

Most people thought the crash of Flight 11 was an accident until seventeen minutes later, when United Airlines Flight 175 flew into the South Tower at 9:03 a.m. The plane came in at an angle, destroying most of floors 77 to 85. Hundreds of people were killed instantly, including all sixty-five people on board the airplane. Incredibly, one of the South Tower's three stairwells survived the impact, and eighteen people from above the 77th floor were able to make their way down and around the impact zone to safety. Another 614 people who never found the open staircase were not as fortunate.

The Twin Towers had been built to withstand hurricane-force winds, and they had sprinklers and fire hydrants on each floor. But no one could have anticipated what thousands of gallons of burning jet fuel would do to the towers' internal steel structures. City officials were convinced the buildings wouldn't fall— right up until the moment that they did. Despite being hit second, the South Tower was the first to collapse at 9:59 a.m. The North Tower followed at 10:28 a.m., just 102 minutes—less than two hours—from the moment the first plane had struck. Both towers came almost straight down, their debris damaging buildings for blocks. Later that day, the forty-seven-story 7 World Trade Center collapsed due to damage it sustained when the North Tower came down.

An estimated 14,000 to 17,500 people were in the

World Trade Center complex at the time of the attacks—far fewer than would have been in the buildings if the planes had hit later in the day. Miraculously, most people below the impact zones survived.

The number of dead and wounded is still horrifying: 2,977 victims died in the attacks, and an estimated 25,000 more people were injured. The number of dead includes 343 New York City firefighters who were working to rescue people in and around the towers when they came down. Sixty officers from the New York City Police Department and the Port Authority Police Department died in the collapse, as did eight emergency medical technicians and paramedics. Hundreds more rescue workers who worked at Ground Zero that day and in the months that followed have since died, many of them from exposure to toxins at the site. The September 11 attacks remain the deadliest incident for firefighters and law enforcement officials in the history of the United States, and the single deadliest terrorist attack in human history.

Like Brandon, there were children in the Twin Towers at the time of the attacks. All those children survived. Eight of the passengers on the planes were children, however, and they all died in the crashes. They ranged in age from two to eleven years old.

Twenty minutes before the South Tower came down, a third plane, American Airlines Flight 77, crashed into the Pentagon, the headquarters of the United States Department of Defense, in Arlington, Virginia, right outside Washington, DC. The impact killed all 64 people on board, including the five hijackers, and another 125 victims in the building.

The fourth plane, United Airlines Flight 93, was hijacked just after the second plane hit the South Tower. When the passengers on Flight 93 used phones on the planes to call their families, they learned about the attacks on the Twin Towers and on the Pentagon, and they knew their plane would be next. Monitoring the situation from the safety of Air Force One, the special plane that carries the president of the United States, President George W. Bush made the difficult decision to order F-16 fighter jets to shoot down Flight 93 if it got close to a major city.

Before the fighter pilots had to carry out that unimaginably terrible task, a group of brave passengers on board Flight 93 stormed the cockpit to try to wrestle control of the airplane away from the terrorists. During the struggle—right around the time the South Tower was collapsing—Flight 93 crashed into a field near Shanksville, Pennsylvania, killing everyone on board. To this day, no one knows the exact target of Flight 93. The plane was headed toward Washington, DC, and the White House and the Capitol were likely possibilities. Whatever the terrorists' target was, the forty passengers and crew of Flight 93 stopped another deadly attack and may have saved many more lives by sacrificing their own.

THE TERRORISTS

All nineteen of the terrorists were men. Fifteen were from Saudi Arabia, and all were from middle- and upper-class families in the Middle East. Most of their mothers and fathers had no idea their sons had become terrorists. The young men had been recruited, radicalized, and trained by al Qaeda, a militant Islamic extremist group founded in 1988 by Osama bin Laden and a number of other men who had fought together in the Soviet-Afghan War.

Born into a wealthy Saudi Arabian family, Osama bin Laden received an elite education before moving to Pakistan. There, with support from the American Central Intelligence Agency, bin Laden funded and trained mujahideen fighting in the Soviet-Afghan War. When that war ended, bin Laden founded al Qaeda to drive other "infidels" from Muslim lands, overthrow Arab governments supported by Western countries, and institute an extremist version of Islam as the law of the land. To achieve those goals, al Qaeda began a campaign of bombings and suicide attacks against military and civilian targets that continues to this day.

Osama bin Laden and the al Qaeda leadership chose the hijackers from the ranks of their organization and gave them their targets. Five of the hijackers moved to the United States over a year before the attacks, taking piloting classes and practicing on flight simulators. The other hijackers, the ones who would provide the "muscle" in subduing the crew and passengers, arrived in the US in early 2001. Bin Laden paid for all their housing and training, but it was the hijackers themselves who chose the day and the flights.

In the days after 9/11, when the United States was determined to find out who had planned the attacks, attention focused on Afghanistan, where Osama bin Laden and al Qaeda were headquartered.

THE WAR IN AFGHANISTAN

Afghanistan is roughly the size of Texas, and sits in a strategically important location between Europe and Asia. As Reshmina notes, the country has been invaded over the centuries by everyone from Alexander the Great to the United Kingdom.

The Soviet Union invaded Afghanistan in 1978 and finally withdrew in 1989. Then came a deadly civil war, after which the Taliban came to power. Despite Afghanistan's desperate need for help after so many years of war, the Taliban refused any international assistance. They created what they called a "pure Islamic society," which in reality was an authoritarian culture based on an extremist interpretation of Islamic law. They instituted restrictions on women and girls, made prayer required, and punished thieves by cutting off their hands or feet. Music and television were outlawed, and movie theaters were closed and turned into mosques. The Taliban held no elections either, claiming to rule by divine right.

The Taliban's strict religious laws and hatred of outsiders were a perfect fit for al Qaeda, and in 1996 Osama bin Laden moved his headquarters and training camps there. When evidence pointed to al Qaeda as the perpetrators of the 9/11 attacks, the United States demanded that Afghanistan's Taliban government close every terrorist camp in the country and hand over bin Laden. When the Taliban refused, the United States invaded Afghanistan, joined by a coalition of countries that included the United Kingdom, Canada, Australia, and Germany. Relying heavily on anti-Taliban Afghan rebels on the ground and superior international air power, the United States and its allies swept to a quick and easy victory by December 2001, defeating the Taliban and al Qaeda without the loss of a single American life.

But Osama bin Laden remained elusive, slipping away across the border into Pakistan before he could be captured. It took another ten years, but bin Laden was eventually found in a compound in Pakistan in 2011 by a team of Navy SEALs. They shot and killed bin Laden, then dumped his body at sea.

TODAY

In 2004, Afghanistan formed a new, democratically elected government supported by the US and its allies. The change in leadership has brought more freedom for women and girls, better health care, and better education. But life in Afghanistan is still difficult. Almost half the population lives below the poverty line, making it the second poorest country in the world. Less than 15 percent of Afghanistan's land can support farming, and roughly 35 percent of the population does not have access to clean drinking water. There are very few hospitals in Afghanistan, and Afghan doctors often lack proper training and equipment. Life expectancy at birth is among the lowest of any country.

The Taliban, defeated but not eliminated, has continued its fight against the new Afghan government and its Western allies. Since the beginning of the war, almost 2,500 American soldiers have died, and more than 22,000 more have been wounded. By contrast, more than 65,000 members of the Afghan National Army (the US's allies in Afghanistan) have died, and an estimated 70,000 Taliban insurgents have been killed. Even more striking, more than 40,000 Afghan civilians have died—that we know of. According to the United Nations, 2018 was the single deadliest year for civilians in Afghanistan in a decade. And not all civilian deaths are caused by the Taliban. In 2019, the United States and their Afghan allies accounted for 29 percent of all civilian casualties, 30 percent of which were children.

To escape the fighting, many Afghans choose to flee over the border into neighboring countries, like Pakistan and Iran. According to the United Nations Refugee Agency, 2.7 million of the world's 25.9 million refugees in 2019 came from Afghanistan, ranking second only to Syria. Half a million Afghans qualify as internally displaced persons—people who were forced by war to abandon their homes and now live in makeshift refugee camps in their own country.

Though US combat operations in Afghanistan officially ended in 2014, thousands of American soldiers remain in the country to train, advise, and assist the Afghan military. On-again, off-again negotiations between the US and the Taliban have promised an end to the fighting, but no end has come. The War in Afghanistan is now officially the longest war in US history.

Life in America has also changed a great deal since

9/11. Shortly after the attacks, police and rescue workers from all across the country went to New York City to help search for survivors at Ground Zero, and blood donations increased. Unfortunately, hate crimes also rose sharply. Many Muslims and South Asians reported harassment, and mosques and Muslim businesses were vandalized and set on fire.

In the months and years that followed 9/11, a number of American rights and privacies were curtailed or lost in the name of safety. The Patriot Act, enacted in October 2001, gave law enforcement agencies the freedom to search homes and businesses, read private emails, and listen in on phone calls, all without having to get permission from a judge. Airline travel has changed too; thanks to the newly created Transportation Security Administration (TSA), passengers traveling by plane now face carry-on restrictions, complicated screenings, and invasive pat-downs.

Nearly twenty years after 9/11, the United States remains in a national state of emergency. The World Trade Center was rebuilt, with the new One World Trade Center building officially replacing the Twin Towers in 2014. The building's height—1,776 feet—commemorates the year the United States Declaration of Independence was signed. The National September 11 Memorial & Museum, opened in 2011, is nearby. Two square reflecting pools sunk into the ground mark the outlines of where the Twin Towers once stood, and museum buildings house artifacts recovered from the wreckage, including twisted steel beams, damaged stairs, and parts of the hijacked airplanes. Today the memorial and museum receive nearly ten million visitors a year.

Though I thought I was ready to confront my own memories and emotions from 9/11, *Ground Zero* proved to be one of the most emotionally difficult books I've written. 2021 will mark the twenty-year anniversary of 9/11. Will it also mark the twenty-year anniversary of the War in Afghanistan? Time will tell.

One way or another, we still live in a world reshaped and redefined by what happened in those 102 frightful minutes on a bright blue September morning in 2001. And I believe it's more important than ever for new generations to understand how we got from there to where we are today.

Alan Gratz
May 2020

ACKNOWLEDGMENTS

Huge thanks to my amazing editor, Aimee Friedman, who first suggested I tackle a book about 9/11 and helped me figure things out every step of the way. Thanks too to my ever-supportive publisher, David Levithan; to copy editor Shari Joffe and proofreaders Jody Corbett, Jackie Hornberger, and Jessica White; and everyone behind the scenes at Scholastic: Ellie Berger, president of trade publishing; Lauren Donovan in publicity; Erin Berger, Rachel Feld, and Julia Eisler in marketing; Lizette Serrano, Emily Heddleson, Michael Strouse, Matthew Poulter, and Danielle Yadao in school and library marketing and conventions; Aimee's associate editor, Olivia Valcarce; Josh Berlowitz, Elizabeth Krych, Erin O'Connor, Leslie Garych, JoAnne Mojica, and everyone in production; Yaffa Jaskoll for the terrific cover and interior layout; map artist Jim McMahon; Jazan Higgins, Stephanie Peitz, Jana Haussmann, Kristin Standley, Robin Hoffman, and everyone with the clubs and fairs; Jennifer Powell and her team in rights and co-editions; Alan Smagler, Elizabeth Whiting, Jackie Rubin, Savannah D'Amico, Dan Moser, Nikki Mutch, Sue Flynn, Chris Satterlund, Roz Hilden, Terribeth Smith, Randy Kessler, Betsy Politi, and everyone in sales; Lori Benton, John Pels, and Paul Gagne for their amazing work, as ever, on *Ground Zero* the audiobook; and all the sales reps and fairs and clubs reps across the country who work so hard to tell the world about my books.

Special thanks to Sergeant Matthew Peterson, who served in the US army in Afghanistan, and to Hanif Sufizada, coordinator of education and outreach programs for the University of Nebraska Omaha's Center for Afghanistan Studies, for reading the chapters with Reshmina and Taz and giving me notes. Your comments were invaluable. Any mistakes that remain are my own.

Thanks as always to my great friend Bob. And big thanks to my literary agent, Holly Root at Root Literary, and to my publicists and right-hand women, Lauren Harr and Caroline Christopoulos at Gold Leaf Literary—the work you do allows me to do the work I do. And thanks again to all the teachers, librarians, and booksellers out there who put my books into the hands of young readers—you're awesome!

Last but never least, much love and thanks to my wife, Wendi, and my daughter, Jo.

It's not us against the world; it's all of us, working together, for each other.

ABOUT THE AUTHOR

Alan Gratz is the *New York Times* bestselling author of several acclaimed books for young readers, including *Refugee*, a New York Times Notable Book and an Amazon, Kirkus Reviews, and Publishers Weekly Best Book of the Year; *Allies*, recipient of four starred reviews and an Amazon Best Book of the Year; *Grenade*, the 2018 Freeman Book Award winner; *Projekt 1065*, a Kirkus Reviews Best Book of the Year; *Prisoner B-3087*, winner of eight state awards and included on YALSA's 2014 Best Fiction for Young Adults list; and *Code of Honor*, a YALSA 2016 Quick Pick for Reluctant Young Adult Readers. Alan lives in North Carolina with his wife and daughter. Look for him online at alangratz.com.

Heart-pounding action.
High stakes danger.
Read more books from Alan Gratz!

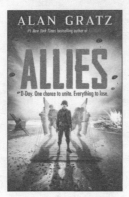

Fire. Ice. Flood.
Three climate disasters.
Four kids fighting
to survive.

It's June 6, 1944: D-Day.
Can the world come
together to defeat evil?

Three different kids.
Three different time
periods. One mission
in common: escape.

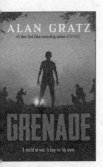

Two soldiers collide
during World War II's
Battle of Okinawa, and
everything changes.

In Nazi Germany,
a boy joins the Hitler
Youth . . . as a spy.

Ten concentration
camps. It's something
no one could imagine
surviving. But it is
what Yanek Gruener
has to face. Based on an
incredible true story.

With his life on the
line, can Kamran clear
his brother's name
by unlocking a series
of secret codes?